DEAD RECKONING

by Marilinne Cooper

CHAPTER ONE

Tyler opened one eye and peered through the haze of mosquito netting surrounding the bed. He tried to read the time on the small alarm clock that sat on the nightstand, but although he could see a couple of flies walking across the top of its black metal frame, he could not make the numbers on the face come into focus.

Damn. He hated this failing middle–aged eyesight thing that seemed to happen to people in their forties. If he lived somewhere with giant discount stores he would go buy one of those clocks with extra–big numbers. But on a craggy hillside above Grand Anse Beach, there wasn't much chance of that.

What difference did it make what time it was anyway. He didn't have to be at work until four. Rolling over onto his back, he kicked the damp and twisted top sheet off his body. From the rising temperature of the air in the tiny bedroom he guessed it was at least noon. Through the open louvers of the window he could hear the scuffling and clucking of chickens roaming the yard. His ears could pick up the sound of a radio talk show from the house across the way where Miss Valerie, his eighty–year–old landlady, lived. In the distance he could make out the syncopated bass line of a reggae tune, probably blasting from one of the minibuses that ran up and down the main road. If he listened carefully he might even be able to hear the raucous laughter of the domino players at the local rum shop.

A loud rapping on the wall outside the window brought him out of his reverie. He realized this was what must have woken him in the first place.

"Tyler, mon! Wake up!" It was young Jimbo, the teenage son of Tyler's employer.

"I'm up. I'm up. What's going on?" Tyler pulled the sheet over the lower half of his body and struggled to a sitting position.

"Why you still sleepin', mon? It past lunchtime, you know." Through the glass slats of the window, Tyler caught a flash of Jimbo's white teeth as his face lit up with an infectious grin. "You party too hard last night."

"If I did, it must have been so hard that I can't even remember it." Tyler was not about to explain to a fourteen–year–old why he had trouble getting up in the morning. "Is that what you came by to tell me?"

"No, one lady from England call you at the restaurant. Say she going to call back in an hour. So you better be getting dressed and coming down right away."

"A lady from England? What was her name?" Tyler frowned, wondering who could possibly have tracked him down on the island of Grenada. As far as he knew, only his immediate family in New York was aware of how to reach him by phone. The few others he had remained in touch with contacted him by e–mail, and even those communications were few and far between.

"She not say, mon. She just say it was very important and to tell you she would call back in an hour. You want me to wait and walk wit' you?"

"No, you go on. I'm going to hop in the shower first." Tyler pulled the mosquito netting aside and swung his long legs over the side of the bed. "And Jimbo – I'll owe you big time if you make a fresh pot of coffee before I get there."

As he heard Jimbo's footsteps moving away from the building, Tyler fell back onto the rumpled sheets and closed his eyes. His natural curiosity, that he had worked so hard to suppress in the last five years, had almost gotten to him for a moment. If he knew what was good for him, he would just lay here until the hour had passed and miss the call. It was better not to disturb the sameness of the everyday existence he had made for himself here, the lazy rum–soaked island routine of sunshine and slowness.

There was no one from his days in London that he wanted to hear from. It was the part of his life that he had worked hardest to forget.

He staggered stiffly into the tiny bathroom and stared at his face in the mirror. When he first awoke, he always appeared older than he expected he would. The former laugh lines of his once boyish good looks had now deepened into crevices and wrinkles, urged on by the aging effects of the tropical sun. His thick, curly hair had been bleached nearly blond from afternoons on the beach and the lightened color neatly disguised the gray that was shooting its way through. The same was true of his full beard. He knew he would look younger if he shaved it off, but the truth was he didn't care about his appearance much anymore and it was easier not having to shave. There was no one he needed to impress these days, not even himself.

Okay. He might as well go down to the Papaya Tree and have some coffee and see if she called back. Could be Jimbo had got it wrong and it had not been someone from England at all.

The midday sun was strong and by the time Tyler had reached the restaurant on the beach he was drenched in sweat and ready for a swim. Even after all this time, nothing lifted his spirits as much as a dip in the turquoise waters of the Caribbean. Kicking off his flip–flops and stripping out of his faded t–shirt, he waded through the clear, shallow water near the shore until he could dive under for a swim.

He had not swum ten yards when he heard Jimbo calling his name.

"Tyler! Come now!"

Jimbo was standing on the sand in front of the restaurant holding a portable phone and gesturing frantically.

With a few long strokes he was back on the beach, rising from the sea like a monster, rivulets of water streaming off his body. Jimbo came down to meet him and as he handed over the receiver, he whispered, "She say her name is Amelia, mon."

"Amelia? I don't know any–" Tyler stopped and sighed. "Hello?"

"Is this Tyler Mackenzie?" The accent was definitely British.

"Speaking."

"This is Amelia Rigby. I'm Lucy Brookstone's sister."

Lucy. The one person in England who he might be remotely interested in hearing from, just to know that she was alive and well. "So how is Lucy?" He realized he was being obnoxiously abrupt but he couldn't seem to make himself be otherwise.

"That's what I'm calling about. We've had some rather bad news." Even through the trans–Atlantic fiber optics he could hear her swallowing and hesitating in a way that made his wet skin feel suddenly cold and clammy.

"What's that?"

"Well, apparently Lucy died in a car crash last month."

"Jesus. Shit. I am so sorry. I didn't know."

We didn't know it ourselves until we read the obituary in the paper. It was a terrible way to find out that your own sister was dead. We hadn't been in touch much since she got together with Kip. Actually we'd had a pretty bad falling out when she quit her job and went off with him."

Tyler's head was spinning now with all the news she was giving him. He made his way blindly to a shady spot under a palm tree and sat down on the sand. "I guess I am totally lost here. You're telling me Lucy quit her job with the paper and ran off with that has–been punk rocker?"

"Well, yes, but that was years ago. You haven't spoken to her since then?"

"I haven't spoken to anyone since then. How'd you track me down here anyway?"

"Your parents gave me this number. I wouldn't call you like this, Tyler, but I am desperate." Tyler tried to remember what Lucy's sister looked like. They'd only met once, when Lucy'd taken him to Amelia's for Christmas, but that had been longer ago than he liked to think about. He could vaguely picture a plump little woman with a round, open face, curly fair hair and as many freckles on her body as Lucy had.

"That's okay," he said absently, lost in memories. "Is she still with, I mean *was* she still with Kip?"

"No, I don't think so, but he's not returning my calls. Here's the thing. I haven't been able to find anything out because Lucy wasn't in London when she died. She was on a little island in the Caribbean called..." she stumbled over the name as she tried to pronounce it, "Beck–wee–ay."

"Bequia?" Tyler repeated in astonishment. "But that's just right up from here, in the Grenadines. What the hell was she doing there?" The idea that Lucy had been just a short plane ride away unnerved him even more.

"From what I can gather, I guess Kip has a house on Mustique which is just the next island over. All I know is what I read in the obituary that was printed in the Times." He could hear her sniff and then blow her nose. "I can fax it to you if you want to see it."

"Uh, sure." He thought the Papaya Tree had a fax machine but he wasn't certain. "Or maybe you could email it to me."

"Look, Tyler, the real reason I called is that I need your help. I need you to go to Bequia for me." Amelia seemed to suddenly gain control of her emotions and become very business–like. "I'd go myself except that

I'm eight months pregnant and they won't let me on an overseas airplane."

Tyler hesitated a moment before replying. Going to Bequia was really not in his plans, or lack thereof, for the next month. Nor within his hand–to–mouth budget. "I'm not sure I understand. What exactly do you want me to do there, Amelia?"

"First of all, I'd like to find out what really happened. It all seems so shady to me. It may seem gruesome, but I'd like to know just how Lucy died. I'm also rather surprised that the police or hospital didn't contact me at the time. It took place nearly a month ago."

"Well, things can move kind of slowly down here, particularly bureaucratic –" he began, but she cut him off as she went on.

"And then there's also somebody I need you to find. I know you used to do this kind of work and don't worry, I'll pay all your expenses."

"Used to. Those are the key words, Amelia. Used to. I don't do that kind of work anymore. I'm done with investigating and journalism. That part of my life is over." Tyler could feel the invisible curtain of safety sliding down over his feelings again, the one he had used to protect himself from the remembrance of things past. "I'm sure there's some private detective in London you can hire who would jump at the chance to hop on the next plane to a tropical paradise."

"Please, Tyler. It's really important. I can trust you and you're already in the neighborhood, so to speak." Her voice was beginning to take on an edge of hysteria. "If it was just any old person that I was looking for, it would be one thing, but it's not." She was crying for real now, big gulping sobs.

"I'm really sorry, but I just can't."

"It's her son."

"Whose son?"

"Lucy's. She had a boy who would be almost six by now. We've got to find him. I don't know if he was with her at the time or if he's with Kip now or where he is. I can't seem to find out anything!" Her words were coming out between great gasps for air. "I feel so damn helpless here, blown up like an elephant..."

Tyler was speechless. If Lucy had a child who was nearly six, she would probably have already been pregnant the last time he had seen her. This was all too hard to imagine and he just didn't want to deal with it. It was way too much personal news for someone who had been making a career out of feeling nothing.

"Look, Amelia, I–"

"Please don't say no, Tyler. Just think about it. I don't know what the best way for you to get there is, by boat or by plane, but I will call the airline and get you a round trip ticket to wherever you need to go. I'm not sure you can even fly to an island that small..."

"Yes, you can. But –"

"I'm going to book a ticket for Saturday and pray that you will go. And if you tell me where, I will wire some money or send you a check by Fed Ex. I'm going to trust that you are going to agree to this because at this point there's nothing else I can do." She was calming herself down, making plans that she could believe in to give herself the will to go on. "I'll call this number tomorrow and let you know what flight you are on."

"Amelia, I have a job and a life here! I can't just run off at the drop of a hat!" But even as he said it, Tyler knew it wasn't true. He had no ties to Grenada. He could leave in a heartbeat.

"His name is Tucker."

"Who?"

"My nephew. Lucy's son. Thanks for your help, Tyler. I'll call you tomorrow with the details." Before he could protest again, she hung up the phone.

Tucker. Lucy Brookstone was dead and she'd left behind a son named Tucker.

"De phone call finish, mon?" Jimbo's shadow fell across the sand in front of him. "It bad news?"

"Very bad news." Tyler shook his head in disbelief and stood up. "I think I need a drink."

"Coffee ready, mon." Jimbo took the phone and led the way into the cool, open–air interior of the restaurant.

"Forget the coffee. I mean a real drink."

By his second shot of Mt. Gay rum on ice, Tyler had relaxed enough to allow himself to think. By his third shot, he was almost ready to feel grief. By his fourth shot, he was over that bit of weakness and back to numb, mindless thinking again.

Lucy.

They'd been such good friends, buddies, and co–conspirators before they became lovers. Lucy had rescued him when his relationship with Sarah had ended. Sarah's ideas for long–term commitment had begun to include making a family with him as a father and Tyler had felt as though he was about to suffocate under a blanket of expectation. And then Sarah had found someone else who could give her what Tyler couldn't.

Lucy had taken him away from all that, from the mountains of Vermont, where there was nothing left for him without Sarah. She not only let him move into her flat in London, but had helped him get his career back on track again. Some years before, they'd had a torrid affair during a time when he had spent a couple of weeks in England. Lucy had been the first woman he had known who could keep something like that in perspective. They had remained long–distance comrades of the trade, calling on each other when help was needed, both appreciating the period they had spent together for what it had been, a satisfying point in time and space.

Lucy's high energy and bubbly personality had kept him from sinking into depression in the months after he and Sarah broke up. A foot shorter than he was, she had a thick, curly mane of sunset–colored hair that framed her face and shoulders like a Botticelli angel. Because of her round face and diminutive size, she could pass for a young girl even when she was well into her thirties.

At the time Tyler had sensed that she was still holding a torch for him, but that she knew enough not to press the issue until he was ready. She had made everything easy for him, introducing him to magazine and newspaper editors that she knew, giving him food and lodging until he was able to contribute some money, and mostly forcing him to laugh and have a good time.

During the year that they lived together, Tyler would have to say that they were never really "in love." They were more like best friends who slept together and supported each other.

Tyler had been away in France, doing an expose on the wine–making industry when Lucy had gotten approval to do a story that fulfilled one of her unrealized teenage dreams. She would go on tour with Boneyard, a heavy metal band that had seen its fifteen minutes of fame twenty years earlier, and document what life was like for middle–aged rockers who were now old enough to need reading glasses and have pot bellies and cholesterol problems.

Kip Kingsley, the lead guitarist, had been the heart throb that an adolescent Lucy and all her friends had had a crush on. She had stood outside sold–out concerts for hours, straining to get a glimpse of him, screaming along with the rest of the fans at any sign of his rail–thin physique beneath the signature silver leather jacket, of his shoulder–length straw–blonde hair framing seven earrings in one ear and ten in the other, or of the deep creases in his cheeks that passed for dimples when he smiled and revealed a twinkling diamond filling in one of his front teeth...

When she had called Tyler in Bordeaux to tell him the news, she had sounded as excited as a fifteen–year–old and he could not keep from laughing at her.

"A month, Tyler! A whole month on the road with Kip Kingsley, all expenses paid! This is the assignment of my lifetime!"

"Lucy, they're a bunch of burned–out former drug addicts, who probably have wives and kids now."

"You don't know that! How can you pass judgment on them; you have no idea what they are like now."

There was clearly no reasoning with her so he hadn't bothered. Instead he promised to water the plants and feed the cat until she came home from the tour. Only she never really did come home.

The first time Lucy called him from the road, he knew she had slept with Kip already. When he accused her of it, she had just laughed merrily. He decided to let it slide, clearly it was something she needed to get out her system and they truly had no commitment to each other. The next time he talked to her she was in Moscow, but he couldn't blame the distance he felt from her on the bad phone connection. A week later she rang him from Stockholm and he could hear her clear as a bell. "Damn it, Lucy, don't tell me you've fallen in love with him."

"I've been in love with him most of my life! This is my destiny, Tyler. I've never felt like this about anyone."

It made him sick to his stomach to think about what Lucy's life must be like now and he had to believe he was wrong. He knew her so well, she couldn't be living the shallow existence he was imagining.

He left for the Caribbean on an extended assignment about the VSO, Britain's equivalent to the Peace Corps, and was not around when Lucy returned to London and moved in with Kip. By the time he got back, the flat had been stripped of all her personal belongings and she had left him a note with an address for the rent check and a request to change the gas, phone and electric bills to his name.

Tyler only saw Lucy once after that. It was about a year later when she called, asking him to meet her for lunch at a favorite Italian restaurant of hers. Expecting to see her skeletal and haggard from a life of excess, he was surprised by how good she looked. She was wearing an expensive embroidered vest over a sheer black blouse that was cut low enough to expose an expanse of peach–colored freckles on the swell of her breasts. A slim skirt and high–heeled black boots gave her body a shape he had never noticed before. He couldn't recall ever seeing her in a skirt; in fact, he had rarely known her to wear anything other than jeans and t–shirts. What he had always thought of as her fresh–faced innocence now seemed to be replaced by a new awareness of her sexuality.

At first she kept up an ongoing monologue, telling him stories about famous people she'd met and their yachts and fabulous places she and Kip had eaten, and clubs where they went dancing, and his house in the Caribbean. Through it all he found himself more drawn to how she appeared than what she was saying. After a couple glasses of red wine, he couldn't help but comment on it.

"Lu, I have to say, you look pretty sexy," he blurted out with a boyish grin.

A faint blush came over her cheeks and he could almost see the old Lucy emerge before the new one came to the rescue. "You know what, Tyler? I feel pretty sexy these days." She took a huge swallow of her own wine before continuing. "Kip and I, well, let's just say sex is a big part of our relationship." She laughed, staring off into space for a moment before refocusing on Tyler. "He's taken me to new frontiers, to bridges I never thought I would cross."

"Well, you've certainly crossed a bridge in fashion," he remarked, smoothly steering the conversation away from what seemed to be the awkward place it was heading. "But please don't tell me you have any tattoos."

"Not yet," she said with a mischievous look in her eyes. "But I've been thinking about it."

For a few seconds the warmth of their old camaraderie wrapped itself around them. But the familiarity of it made Tyler suddenly wonder what was going on. "So, Lulu, why are we having lunch today? There must be a reason."

"Always so cynical, Tyler, aren't you?" She winked at him as she refilled both their wine glasses. He could not remember her ever winking at him before. Winking was an affectation that took time to cultivate; as quickly as she had become familiar, Lucy became a stranger again. "Okay, there is something I wanted to talk to you about. I'm quitting my job and there's a story I need you to take over for me."

A swirling fog of obscuring darkness came filtering through Tyler's memory, settling like a heavy velvet curtain over his ability to recall the rest of what happened that afternoon. He was suddenly very aware of the glass in his hand, empty except for a ragged slice of lime. Looking up, he saw the shiny mahogany bar of the Papaya Tree. Beyond the dim interior of the restaurant with its rattan tables and chairs lay the blinding whiteness of the beach and the glistening blue sea.

For the last five years, he'd been successful in shoving his past into a box at the back of his mind, a box that he'd had no plans of ever opening again. He'd had to keep it there to be able to live with himself in the pleasant but pointless existence that was now his life. If he had to deal with this Lucy thing, he probably couldn't keep the rest of it neatly packaged away. And there was no way he was going there again.

The angle of the sun reflecting off the water's surface told him the afternoon was getting on. It was time to start prepping for the evening's meals. Helping himself to another shot of Mt. Gay, he headed for the kitchen.

CHAPTER TWO

After Silvalyn had turned her back to him and her breathing had become deep and even, Tyler found he could not keep Lucy out of his thoughts any longer. He had tried to escape into the abyss of sex, but the primal motions of intercourse only kept his memories at bay for the duration of the act. And really it was the act itself that triggered all kinds of recollections, particularly of the last time he and Lucy had been together.

He opened his eyes and tried to focus on his present reality. As his vision became accustomed to the dark, he could make out the full curves of Silvalyn's body as she lay on her side next to him. He had never been with a woman of Silvalyn's dimensions before coming to Grenada. The women in his life had always been tall and slim or petite and compact until Silvalyn's generous hips had swayed in his direction one night a few years earlier. The girth of her buttocks only dominated her silhouette from behind; immense heavy breasts the size of five pound bags of sugar filled the picture frame as she approached. But there was nothing soft about her. She was strong and solid with perfect posture and a classic African beauty about her face and her whole being. The best part was that she reminded him of no one he had ever known before and nothing from his former life.

It was she who had pursued him. He'd had absolutely no interest in having any sort of relationship with anyone or anything except a liquor bottle. She had nearly carried him back up the hill to his bungalow that first night and then he'd been too drunk to perform. Instead he tried to make it up to her by employing a couple of the half dozen or so sure–fire methods he knew for bringing a woman to orgasm.

Silvalyn had been so grateful at his act of unselfishness that she had nearly cried. It had bonded her to him like guava jelly to peanut butter; there was no way any other woman on Grenada was going to get her hands on him. Or more like his hands on her. Over time she explained to him, and he learned through talking to others as well, that in Caribbean culture, sex was mostly about intercourse and the man. It was a very earthy, animalistic urge of possessing; "love" was not a word one heard frequently in conversation and the way to pleasure a woman was by "win'ing and grin'ing" your member into her.

Silvalyn had two children by two different fathers. She and her offspring all resided at her mother's tiny two–room house, where the kids shared a bed with granny and Silvalyn slept on a cot in the front room where occasionally her younger brother slept on the vinyl settee. She hadn't seen her own father since she was twelve when her mother had thrown him out of the house for trying to force himself on her and her older sisters. When she stayed over at Tyler's she was always gone before sunrise, sometimes with just a few hours of sleep and long before he ever got up.

Theirs was a shallow relationship by Tyler's standards, consisting of little more than sex and then only when Silvalyn took the initiative. They had nothing to talk about and not much in common. By Silvalyn's experience this was completely normal and it suited Tyler just fine. He didn't want a girlfriend who wanted to know everything about him, or wanted to spend every free moment with him or wanted him to pay more attention to her. He wouldn't even care if Silvalyn never showed up in his doorway again, although he had to admit that the physical release of sex was a great escape from his mental anxieties, even if it was only temporary.

There had been one woman in the last few years who had tried to get close to him in the way he had been used to. She was an American, from Massachusetts, and she was vacationing without her husband for a week, staying at one of the all–inclusive resorts at the other end of Grande Anse beach. A delightful older woman, who at one time would have captivated his imagination. She had recognized the lost spirit in him, seen through the hardened exterior that protected his fragile insides, and had tried to draw him out. She had been too curious and asked too many questions, and his resulting reaction was the opposite of what she had intended. From then on he had taken great pains to avoid her until she left the island.

Silvalyn stirred in her sleep and curled into the fetal position. Tyler lightly touched her bare hip – the damp sheen of sweat that had covered their bodies after love–making had dried now, leaving her skin cool beneath his fingers. He pulled the top sheet up from the foot of the bed where it had been kicked to a crumpled heap and gently covered her with it. And recalled his last night with Lucy.

Lucy claimed that she had left the flat in a hurry and, as a result, had forgotten to bring along the file she wanted to give him regarding the story she was handing over.

"Let's just run by there after we're done here. I'd love for you to see the place anyway."

Afterwards he was sure she had planned it all along, but at the time he didn't care. He was intrigued by the new Lucy and wanted to see what was so great about her current lifestyle. He was also upset by her decision to quit her job and told her so half a dozen times in the cab on the way there. "No one loves investigating a story more than you, Lu," he protested. "I know you don't need the steady money anymore, but you could still freelance."

"And I will, if I want to. Now bugger off about it, Tyler. I still care or I wouldn't be handing this story over to you." Although he sensed something odd in the way she said this, he decided to let it slide for the moment. He was feeling a bit hazy from all the wine they had drunk with lunch and was enjoying the blanket of warmth that had settled over the two of them.

"Well, this is hardly what I would call a 'flat'," Tyler laughed as she led him into a massive apartment that took up the top floor of a two–hundred–year–old brick building that had once been a tea–packaging factory. It was now refurbished into expensive lofts and studios for artists and musicians. Clearly the most expensive of all was the "penthouse" where Kip lived with a million–dollar view of the city and where his band rehearsed in separate, soundproof quarters.

"Where is the king?" he asked as she showed him around the large, airy rooms full of ultra–modern furniture. It had a well–designed ambience that was sleek and cold, and completely opposite of the cozy, cluttered little flat that Lucy had left him to inhabit.

"He and the band are in Canada this week on a hunting trip. Strictly a male–bonding thing and as far as I'm concerned, it can stay that way." Lucy made a face as she headed for a bar that spanned one entire end of the living room. "Want another glass of wine?"

"Why do I think you're trying to get me drunk?" he laughed. "Is that the only way I'm going to agree to work on this mysterious story that you're ditching?"

"It may help." She put two glasses on the bar. "Hmmm...Looks like we're out of red. I'll have to go down to the 'wine cellar' and get another bottle. Why don't you take a look at the bedroom?"

"You have a wine cellar in a penthouse?" he called over his shoulder as he walked through the doorway she indicated.

"Not really, just a temperature–regulated closet," she replied, but he barely heard her because of the blood rushing to his head as he stared at the enormous photograph on the bedroom wall.

Larger than life, it was a close–up of a magnificent black woman's face as she took a colossally swollen white man's penis in her mouth. Her eyes were closed and her face was expressionless. Tyler wasn't sure if it was the ultimate in degradation or erotica, but the size of the photograph gave the graphic details an intimacy that seemed to celebrate the act in a way that was both revolting and mesmerizing.

It was placed so that it could be seen both from the bedroom door and from the giant king–size bed. Covered in a beaded and embroidered crimson silk quilt, the bed was made up in sheets printed with a musical score, the idea of which momentarily diverted his attention from the photograph that loomed over all. As he moved to look more closely at the pattern, he realized that there were other photographs of normal dimensions hung around the room. Most of them he would have termed pornography, but there were a few more usual poses of events, including a much younger Kip accepting a Grammy award and the band displaying their catch on a fishing trip.

Clearly, the newest one was in a standing frame on the night table. He picked it up and sat down slowly on the edge of the bed for a closer examination.

It was a picture of Lucy dancing onstage at a concert. The wavy, strawberry blonde tresses of her waist–length hair were brushed out in all their angel–like beauty and hung down around her like Lady Godiva. Because indeed, from what Tyler could make out, Lucy appeared to be naked from her shoulders to the waistband of her low–slung jeans. Her amazing hair was concealing all that needed to be concealed, although the natural curve of one bare breast showed beneath an upraised arm.

He could not imagine her doing such a thing, but the look captured on her face was one of radiant ecstasy, as though she could not be having a better time anywhere else in the world.

"What do you think?"

Startled, Tyler looked up. Lucy was standing in the doorway holding two glasses of red wine. She had taken off her high–heeled boots and stockings and was working her bare toes into the plush loops of the thick carpet.

"Guess it's a side of me you've never seen before, isn't it?" she said sitting down next to him on the luxurious bedcover. He took the glass she offered, quickly swallowing a few mouthfuls before replying.

"Well, let's just say I've never seen that side of you in public. But apparently thousands of others have."

She grinned. "You sound like a stodgy old codger. I've shown more skin on the beach in a bikini. I did it on a dare the first time. Kip thought it was great publicity and that it increased repeat ticket sales." She leaned back on the bed and stretched her bare legs out in front of her, crossing them at the ankles. "I have to admit, it was a bit of a turn–on."

Tyler shook his head and put the photograph back on the nightstand. "You were always one of the most courageous women I've ever known, but I have to say you are surprising the hell out of me here." When he looked back, the huge photograph loomed above her head, distracting him again. "What about the blow–up of the blow job? Someone you know?"

This time she convulsed with laughter and her legs flew apart to maintain her balance as she held her wine high to keep it from spilling. "I have no idea who that is. It's just art," she replied in a mock–sophisticated voice.

"I suppose there is an art to it." Tyler dragged his eyes down from the wall to look at Lucy. His gaze continued to drop to where her short, tight skirt was inching up her now open legs. He realized she wasn't wearing any underwear.

The rest was inevitable. And pretty damn exciting. He had never realized Lucy had such an insatiable appetite for sex, but then this was a Lucy he barely knew, one who had let go of a lifelong obsession with a career in investigative journalism to become the uninhibited girlfriend of a has–been rock star.

At some point in the evening, they pranced naked up to the rooftop garden where they shivered in the damp London air until Lucy got the lid off of the hot tub. Soaking in the steaming water and gazing out over the lights of the city, Tyler realized how exhausted he was and knew it would soon be time to go. It had all been fabulous, but he didn't want to wake up here in the morning and have to face the reality of it. If he left tonight, he could keep it as the fantasy that it had been.

"Okay, it's time, Lulu. Tell me what this important story is you want me to take over."

And so she told him.

As usual, Tyler's memory went into its protective oblivion mode at this point. But that was fine. He had wanted a clear last image of Lucy in his mind and he had it now. And it seemed in the years that followed, her newfound hedonistic lifestyle had caught up with her. First a child, then a breakup and then an untimely youthful death.

Overwhelming sadness swept over him, and he flung himself out of bed and across the room to the outside door. Pulling back the bolt, he breathed in the cooler air of the Caribbean darkness. The sweet smell of night–blooming jasmine filled his lungs.

There was no way he was going on a scavenger hunt for Lucy's child. Even if he was named Tucker Brookstone.

When the Fed Ex envelope arrived from England a few days later, he debated opening it at all. Everyone at the restaurant was buzzing with excitement about it, but he left it sitting on a high shelf behind the bar until long after he had finished working and had laid back a few shots of rum. When the customers had cleared out and no one was left but himself and Cyrus, the bartender, he brought the envelope down off the shelf and stared at it for several minutes.

"Open it up, mon," urged Cyrus. "How can you not open it?"

But to Tyler it was more than just opening an envelope; it was unlocking a door to the past that he had kept firmly shut for the last five years. When he had convinced himself that it wouldn't hurt to look at the contents before he threw them away, he finally tore it open and dumped it onto the bar.

An airline ticket from a London travel agency was clipped to the top of an irregular stack of papers. First was a letter from Amelia thanking him profusely and telling him to check the times on the ticket, as well as the ferry schedule she had downloaded because he would have to take a ferry from St. Vincent to Bequia. And also that she had booked him into the Frangipani Hotel in Port Elizabeth, and that the return portion of his ticket could be changed without a fee for whatever length of time he needed to stay.

Beneath the letter was a copy of Lucy's obituary from the London Times.

"St. Vincent and the Grenadines – Lucille Brookstone, 41, formerly of London, died September 23rd in an auto accident on the island of Bequia. Born in Southampton…" Tyler scanned quickly through the details of Lucy's education and work history. "…She is survived by a sister, Amelia Brookstone Rigby, and her husband, Robert Rigby, two nieces, and by a son, Tucker Brookstone. A memorial service was held September 30th on Bequia and her ashes were scattered at sea. In lieu of flowers or condolences, contributions can be sent to the Sunny Island Primary School, P.O. Box 173, Bequia, St. Vincent and the Grenadines, West Indies."

Placing the obituary aside, he looked at the remaining two items. There were two photographs with a yellow post–it note attached to the first one that read, "These are a few years old, but they're all I have and they may help." Removing the note he looked at the first snapshot in his hand.

It was a picture of a small, slim boy kneeling in the sand on a beach, playing with a bucket and shovel. His full head of blond curls stood in contrast to his bronzed skin; he clearly had not inherited Lucy's fair freckled complexion. He was grinning broadly at the camera, deep dimples showing in his chubby cheeks. Something hung from a cord around his neck, but Tyler could not make out what it was. The pose reminded him of something familiar, a photo of someone else perhaps, but he couldn't place who or where.

The second one filled him with emotion, both sadness and delight at the same time. Here was a close–up of Lucy holding her toddler son, actually laughing and wrestling with him was a more apt description. She seemed to be trying to hold him still on her lap for the photo, their heads next to one another, cheeks touching, her arms wrapped around his chest, holding him against her own. Her bare freckled shoulders appeared behind the boy's mercurial body and gave the impression that perhaps she was not wearing a top. The more he examined the picture, the more he was sure of it. Her long hair was loosely pulled back and out of the way. Her mouth was open as though she was speaking and the lines in her face crinkled as she smiled.

He pushed it away, and picked up the ticket jacket. Tucked into the inside pocket was an international money order for 500 pounds. "Let me know if you need more" said the sticky note on it. The ticket was for Caribbean Star flight 742 leaving Grenada at 7:40 am on Saturday morning. Tyler couldn't remember the last time he'd seen 7:40 am. And he wasn't going to see it now.

So that was that. It was curious that Lucy's relationship to Kip Kingsley was not mentioned in the obituary at all. As he recalled, she had been pictured extensively in the British rags in the early days of her time with him, in that prying paparazzi style of journalism that Lucy herself had hated so much. He wondered where the obituary had come from if her own sister, Amelia, had known nothing about it.

He was wondering way too much. He shoved everything back into the envelope, saving the first photograph for last. There was still something about the picture that disturbed him. He almost felt as though he had seen it before, but that was impossible.

"Last one before I close," Cyrus warned him as he refilled Tyler's glass one more time.

"Thanks, Cyrus. If you want to leave, I'll lock up."

Cyrus accepted his proposition gratefully. Alone with his drink, he stared at the cute little boy mugging for whoever was taking his picture. In the background he could see a sarong and a straw bag next to a pair of flip–flops. Turning the photo over, he had another sudden jolt of emotion as he saw Lucy's handwriting. "Tucker at age 3 on Macaroni Beach, Mustique."

He didn't know why it touched him so. It was just a simple message, the recording of a moment in time, something every mother did.

And then with a heart–wrenching jolt, he knew what the picture reminded him of. And he also knew there was no question that he would be on that plane on Saturday morning, even if he had to stay up all night to make it.

CHAPTER THREE

The ferry workers were just starting to unhook the massive chains that held the Admiral II to the dock as Tyler sprinted from his taxi and leaped up the loading ramp into the hold. As he climbed the stairs to the upper deck, he could feel his heart pounding faster than usual and when he reached the top, he paused to catch his breath. He was not used to racing to catch anything. His life on Grenada had been a slow amble where nothing was so important it couldn't wait until tomorrow.

But the dock in Kingstown was not a picturesque place to spend the two and a half hours he would have had to wait until the next ferry departed for Bequia. It was a typical working wharf scene; the smell of rotting garbage and diesel fuel, the rough shouting of the dock hands as they lowered cranes and booms of cargo onto pallets, the vendors selling stale packets of crisps and tepid orange sodas, all mixed with the rising heat of the morning sun.

He was glad his taxi driver from the airport had suggested he might want to make a run for the nine a.m. boat. He was also glad his only luggage was an overstuffed daypack that he had carried on the plane. If he'd had to wait for his bags and then go through customs, he would have had to spend the next few hours sitting on one of the concrete abutments that he could now see receding into the distance as the ferry chugged out of the harbor.

His quick fifteen minute tour of St. Vincent left him with the impression that as a country, it was not very different from Grenada. Turquoise and pink wooden houses nestled into steep green hills. Narrow winding roads along which pedestrians risked their lives as they headed for local rum shops and markets. A few glass and concrete mansions standing out among the indigenous and easy–going Third World poverty.

Long benches ran the length of both sides of the ferry and filled the middle of the deck as well. He found himself a seat – on his left was a large woman in a bright fuchsia dress and matching visor who was already snoring, on his right was a skinny old man who stunk of sweat and rum. Resting his legs on his pack, he settled in and took inventory of the rest of his fellow travelers.

Rather than the sea of dark faces he anticipated, he was surprised to find that there were quite a few people as white as he was. Well, that was not entirely accurate he realized, looking down at the long, very brown limbs stretched out in front of him. After his years in the Caribbean, his skin was darker than many of the West Indians he knew. But nonetheless, he found it interesting how many non–natives had braved the dock in Kingstown to head for the small out–island ten miles away.

Some of them looked like yachties in shorts and deck shoes and some were clearly retirees living out their days in hard–won paradise. There was a youngish trio he pegged as backpackers, Germans he realized when he heard them speaking. There was a very pale, exhausted–looking American woman with her ten year old daughter –they both wore sneakers and long pants that were rolled up to the knees and had jackets tied around their waists. Definitely right off the plane, still wearing their cold weather clothing.

He turned his attention to the Vincentians as he thought they were called. A teenage mother wearing a tight jean skirt sat looking out to sea; the infant on her lap was dressed in her matching Sunday best, from the pale yellow booties to the yellow barrettes in the tiny braids on her head. Tyler was fascinated by the miniscule gold hoops in her little ears. A man with long dreadlocks and a rainbow striped tam was polishing a black coral bracelet. Two middle–aged men leaned over the rail, talking animatedly to each other in a patois too fast for Tyler to understand.

"One way or round trip?"

He looked up to see one of the ferrymen, wearing a change apron, carrying a hole puncher and waiting impatiently for his response.

"Uh, one way, I guess."

"Fifteen EC." Tyler counted out the Eastern Caribbean currency with which he was intimately familiar by now.

The boat had cleared the harbor and was beginning a more steady roll as it cut through the waves in the channel between the two islands. Tyler closed his eyes and let the rhythmic rocking of the ferry lull him into the netherworld of being neither here nor there, but on the way.

It was the first time he had left his world on Grenada since he had arrived five years earlier. He had not gone home even once, not for Thanksgiving, not for Christmas, not for his parents' fiftieth wedding anniversary. He rationalized that he was not really leaving his universe, he was still in the Grenadines, and although he was actually in a different country, the culture was virtually the same.

He did not want to admit to himself how good it felt to be traveling again, to be investigating something, no matter how oddly personal it was. By this evening he would probably have the answers Amelia needed and be on his way to the familiar, comfortable haze of Mt. Gay and lime juice.

The rolling of the boat on the waves rocked him like a hammock in the wind and suddenly he found he could not keep his eyes open. On a normal day, he would not even have gotten out of bed for a few hours yet. Silvalyn had been his alarm clock this morning. She ensured he would stay awake by sobbing that he was leaving her and never coming back and then moaning that he should take her with him. Seymour, the owner of the Papaya Tree, had told Tyler to take as much time off as he wanted, seeing as he hadn't taken a vacation in the four and a half years he had worked there.

"If we figure one week a year, I owe you at least a month's holiday," Seymour had laughed. "Go, mon. Put a smile on dat gloomy face of yours. Bequia is a fine place to party."

Tyler hadn't explained to anyone why he was going. He didn't explain much of anything to anyone anymore. The less they knew about his previous life, the easier it was to go on with his current existence.

Suddenly the engine slowed to a chug and he opened his eyes. The ferry was making its way through a harbor that, by Tyler's standards, was very crowded. Port Elizabeth had a quiet, protected anchorage that clearly made it very appealing to yachts and charters seeking a quiet place to moor for a few days or a few months, or by the look of some of the boats, permanently. Before they drew closer to shore, he caught a glimpse of two smaller pristine crescents of sand to the right of the main bay that looked like picture–perfect palm–lined beaches.

Although the ferry was still turning around to back up to the dock, most of the passengers were already crowding towards the steep stairway leading off the upper deck. Tyler leaned over the side railing instead, checking out the lay of the town. The buildings that lined the harborside road were colorful and seemed well–cared for. A bevy of minibuses and island "taxis" waited for the ferry's arrival. The taxis were actually pickup trucks with benches around the three sides of the back under a canvas roof. In a shady grove of almond trees, the drivers of these vehicles lounged, scoping out the passengers for possible fares.

Then, as soon as the gears of the loading ramp began to grind their loud familiar song, these men sprang to their feet and headed quickly to greet the newcomers.

Tyler wasn't sure how far his hotel was and didn't want to be taken for an unnecessary ride by an overeager taxi driver. "Where is the Frangipani?" he asked one of the teenage mothers disembarking with him.

"Frangi right down dat way, jus' follow de walkway," she said nodding her head to the right.

"It not far, you cahn't miss it," another local woman assured him. "You don' need a taxi if it all de bag you are carrying."

It felt good to be able to stride confidently through crowds on the jetty and ignore the hustle of drivers looking for a fare. Port Elizabeth was bustling with Saturday morning activity, but he headed away from it, down the picturesque walkway the girl had indicated. On one side of the road were colorful shops in West Indian style buildings; a bookstore with an internet café above it, a bakery, a tourist shop selling brilliant batiked sarongs and other clothing. On the other side, along the sidewalk, vendors were set up in the shade of the shoreline trees selling fresh fruits and vegetables, black coral jewelry and artwork.

Within minutes he was walking a narrow cement path along a stone retaining wall that followed the random edge of the harbor, and moving even further from the center of town. He was not alone; he passed other people in pairs or small groups, and occasionally someone solo like himself. The turquoise water lapped softly against the shore and then back to the anchored yachts that seemed to constitute quite a bit of the living space of Admiralty Bay.

By the time he had reached the Frangipani a few moments later, he had already begun to feel the magnetic pull of this charming island. As he stepped off the walkway and into the open patio of the hotel's restaurant, he shook himself slightly to get rid of the feeling. There was no room for romantic attractions anymore in his existence. He was here to do a job, not a find a new life.

But as he moved in the direction of the office, it was hard to keep his eyes from straying to the barman who was setting up for the midday shift and to keep his mind from wondering what it would be like if...

Ten minutes later he had unpacked his daypack and was admiring the view from his balcony. Despite the fact that his room was in one of the newer buildings behind the century–old main building, it had plenty of character. The walls were made of stone and the wooden louvered windows, ceiling fan and mosquito net ensured he would have the classic Caribbean comfort he had grown accustomed to.

His instincts were telling him to sink into the padded lounge chair and take a nap or head to the bar and quench his mid–morning thirst with some Mt. Gay on the rocks. But he fought his basic nature and decided to see if he could get his work done quickly before he gave in to his need for escapism. Slipping the Fed Ex envelope back into his pack, he headed down to the office for directions to the police station.

He could not remember the last time he had dealt with the police in any country, other than customs agents. He thought maybe it had been a speeding ticket in Vermont, an easy, slow–talking country cop with a phony but pleasant expression on his face.

The man he was dealing with now might as well have been a robot for the emotion he was showing. He obviously had not been trained in the modern concept of catching more flies with honey than salt. Before he even knew why Tyler was there, his manner was immediately intimidating. He stood like a flagpole behind a concealing counter, the high collar of his red uniform jacket a militant warning to all who dared to enter here.

"What can I do for you?" His voice was low and controlled.

Tyler cleared his throat, wishing desperately that he had stopped for that shot of rum. "I was hoping that somebody could help me with obtaining some information regarding an accident that happened here a few months ago."

"Accident? What kind accident you are talking about?"

"A car crash. Hold on a sec." He put the Fed Ex envelope on the counter and retrieved Lucy's obituary from it. "See here, September 23rd."

The man in the red jacket studied the copy of the newspaper clipping for a very long time, a deeper frown spreading across his face. "Mack, come look at dis out here," he called over his shoulder. From somewhere in the recesses of the building, Mack appeared. "You know anyt'ing about dis accident?"

A clone of the first cop, Mack shook his head as he checked out the obituary. "I don't remember any accident. You knew this person?" he said looking up at Tyler.

"Yes, I did. Don't you have any records you can look in?"

"Oh, sure, we have records, but something like this I would remember. We don't have very many accidents on Bequia. Maybe because we don't have very many vehicles." A ghost of a grin flew across Mack's lips before he resumed his proper police demeanor.

"Do you mind if we check the records? Just to make sure." Tyler had lived in the Caribbean long enough to know how impossibly hard it could be at times dealing with the local bureaucracy. Matters that could be cleared up in a few minutes in other countries might take weeks in the islands of the Lesser Antilles.

"Yes, we can, but I know that I am not wrong." Mack's accent was somewhat more cultured than usual, which gave him an air of educated authority that put Tyler in his place. Retrieving a log book from beneath the counter, he plopped it down with a resounding smack and began to flip back through the flimsy handwritten pages.

"Here we are, 23 September, there are no vehicle accidents reported. In fact the only accident in the week before is a Mrs. Olivierre's flat tire reported on the road to Industry. And it seems we need to go back to the last week of August when a rental car driven by one German fellow mashed up the front left fender of Alvin's taxi as he came out of the Gingerbread. To my knowledge, nobody has died in an auto accident in the last several years. You don't know what kind of car she was in?"

Tyler shook his head. "This is all we know," he said indicating the obituary. "Maybe they got the island wrong. What about the memorial service? Could we check into that?"

"You would have to ask at the church. Maybe they got the cause of death wrong. Perhaps the hospital would know." Mack looked at the obituary again. "But this place, Sunny Island Primary School, now that is a real place. Down in Lower Bay, right, Simon? Maybe they would know something."

"It not open on de weekend," Simon interjected sullenly.

Tyler stood still for a moment, dazed by this unexpected turn of events. "Look," he said at last. "I've been sent here to try to find Lucy Brookstone's son. Have you ever seen this boy?" He pulled out the photographs Amelia had sent him. Tucker's face beamed up at them.

The two men studied the picture until finally Simon commented, "Him look like every white boy come to Bequia."

33

"How about her?" Tyler asked desperately, indicating the other snapshot that included Lucy. "Ever seen her?"

"Yes, her I have seen." Mack nodded vigorously. "But I don't remember when, not for a while now. She come to town sometimes to shop; I think she stay down to Lower Bay. Is she the one who die?"

"Yes, she's the one. So at least we know she was here." Tyler exhaled his breath slowly, not sure what to do next. "Maybe the newspaper got it wrong. Happens all the time, actually. Maybe the accident happened on St. Vincent but since she was living here, the story got confused."

"Maybe so." Mack pursed his lips thoughtfully.

"Can you call over there and find out?" Of course they could, but Tyler knew he had to pose it as a question.

"We can do so," Simon mumbled in his low voice. "But getting an answer will take some time. Office busy over Kingstown way."

Tyler hoped he didn't mean days. "Like how long?" he asked trying not to show his impatience.

"We can maybe know later today, but I don't know, you know. Could be tomorrow."

"Where are you staying?" asked Mack. "We can phone you and let you know."

He gave them his name and his room number at the Frangipani and then stepped back out into the street feeling totally discouraged. What difference did it make where the accident had occurred? It didn't put him any closer to finding Tucker Brookstone.

The midday sun made the asphalt roads of downtown Port Elizabeth radiate heat like a pizza oven. He needed food, he needed alcohol and then he needed a swim to clear his mind. He stopped for a beer and a roti at a small restaurant along the harbor. The local variation of curried vegetables and meat inside a baked pastry crust was always a filling and inexpensive meal.

With another frosty Heineken in hand, he followed the walkway back to his hotel.

Considering all the runoff from the village streets and the effulge of the yachts, the bay, although beautiful and clear, was probably not a savory place for swimming. When he asked at the front desk, he was given instructions to follow the walkway to where it ended at a path that went over a cliff to Princess Margaret Beach, one of the perfect crescents of sand he had seen from the ferry. Stopping at his room for his swim shorts, he deadheaded for the beach.

He was opening the door to the street when suddenly there was a blinding flash of light and a deafening noise. Tyler was knocked backwards off his feet onto the tile floor of the entranceway. A voice was screaming "No! No!" over and over again and then he realized it was his own voice and....

"Hey, man, you okay?"

Tyler shuddered and sat up with a start. He was sitting on a beach and the dark silhouette of someone was standing over him, shading his face from the sun. Sweat was dripping out of every pore of his body, but not from the intense heat of the afternoon. He'd been sound asleep, dreaming in the middle of the day, having the recurring nightmare he'd spent the last five years pushing deeper and deeper inside the recesses of his subconscious.

"Yeah, I'm fine. I was just dreaming..." he said faintly as his rescuer moved to one side.

"I guess you were. You were shouting and shaking. I thought you were having some kind of a seizure."

Tyler could see now that he was a young, golden—haired man with a thin face and small pointed goatee and that he was not alone. His companion was a very brown wisp of a girl in a faded bikini top and a ragged sarong.

"No, I'm fine." Tyler assured him, trying to steady his trembling arms and legs. "But thanks for waking me."

"No problem." The two walked towards a small dinghy that was beached on the edge of the sand and then proceeded to push it into the water and hop in. He watched them row it out to a small sailboat that was moored a few hundred yards from shore. It was probably no more than thirty feet long with a tiny cabin and it was flying the Swedish flag.

Sailing the world, he mused. He wondered what it would be like to be surrounded by nothing but water for days at a time, with only a few planks and some sailcloth as your life support system. And what would you keep between you and your nightmares when the supply of rum ran out?

Shuddering at the thought, he stood up unsteadily and made his way slowly into the calm turquoise bay. The warm water soothed his frayed nerves and cleared the fog from his brain. He looked up and down the length of Princess Margaret Beach. Other than a couple of other clusters of bathers, the sand was deserted. In the shade of a mangrove tree, a tired–looking local sat with a cooler of drinks but it didn't look like he would be making much money today.

Feeling sorry for the drink–vendor and himself, Tyler bought a Hairoun beer, brewed on St. Vincent, for the scenic walk over the cliff back to town. The beer was fine for quenching his thirst, but he needed something stronger to bury his dreams.

He had just settled onto a bar stool to take his first sip of Mt. Gay and lime juice on ice, when he heard his name being called. He turned to see the woman who worked the hotel desk coming towards him.

"Mr. Mackenzie, you had a call from the police a little while ago."

"Oh, thank you. Did they leave a number to call them back?"

"No, they left a message." She read from a piece of paper in her hand. "They said 'tell Mr. Mackenzie no auto accident on St. Vincent on or around September 23rd involving one Lucy Brookstone or any other white woman'." She looked up at him questioningly. "Do you know what that means?"

Although he nodded yes, his mind was screaming no. If there had been no accident, then how did Lucy die? Or was she dead at all? Or what was really going on and what was he doing here?

It was too much to contemplate without a few shots of rum. Knocking back the first one, he pushed his glass back across the bar for another.

At sunset, the Frangipani filled up with yachties and a handful of locals for a lively happy hour on their patio by the harbor. When they all drifted away, Tyler was still at the bar, joined now by a couple of blondes from Atlanta who could keep up a lively conversation without noticing he didn't say much. They tried to talk him into going on a day cruise to Mustique with them the next day, but he declined, mumbling excuses about having to find a place called Lower Bay.

"Oh, Lower Bay is beautiful," one of them gushed. "And tomorrow is Sunday when they have the barbecue and the band at De Reef so there should be plenty of action."

"Maybe we should go there instead and blow off Mustique until Monday," the other suggested and before he knew it they had made plans to meet him the next afternoon in Lower Bay.

Feigning a need to relieve himself, he slipped away and stumbled back to his room. He should probably call Amelia and tell her what he had learned, but it was the middle of the night in England and besides, he hadn't really learned much anyway. And he certainly hadn't found out where Tucker Brookstone was.

37

When he stretched out on the bed and tried to sleep, he found that, despite his exhaustion and the amount of alcohol he had consumed, he still could not relax. He was sorry that he had not given in to the blonde who had been coming on to him. Some mindless sex on an island away from home would probably be just the ticket.

Mindless sex with a nameless blonde from the bar? Who had he become? A vagabond expatriate who couldn't remember his last haircut and whose ancient khaki shorts were held together with a safety pin and almost worn through in the butt. A former award–winning investigative journalist who drowned most of his paycheck each week in a bottle of Barbados rum so he wouldn't have to think about who he had been.

And a grieving ex–lover who thought he just might be able to find some meaning in his life again.

CHAPTER FOUR

"How much for the ride, man?" Tyler asked as the water taxi slowed to an idle in what appeared to be the calmest waters of Lower Bay.

"Ten EC," was the low–pitched response from the driver who wore dark glasses and kept his dreadlocks stuffed into a multi–colored crocheted beret.

Handing him the money, Tyler held his flip–flops and his backpack high as he leaped out into the shallow surf and waded ashore.

"You want me to check you later for a ride back?" the Rasta called over the sound of the outboard motor.

Tyler shrugged. "I don't know how long I'm staying. Thanks anyway."

He watched as the brightly painted skiff took off at a tear, creating a huge wake as it made a large circle and headed back to town. The water taxi equivalent of "burning rubber", he thought amusedly, and then hopped quickly to shore as the growing waves lapped at the edge of his shorts.

The length of the Lower Bay beach lay before him, a half mile of soft sand nestled into steep green hillsides dotted with an eclectic variety of dwellings. A flat road ran a few feet inland from the beach, but at either end it abruptly became a precipitous incline as it rose out of the valley that protected the little village. Tyler had never been to the South Pacific, but there was something about the ambience of the scene that brought to mind the image of a peaceful Polynesian island.

As he walked along the shoreline with the light surf swirling around his ankles, he had to remind himself that he was not just here on holiday, he had a job to do. At one time he would have relished the opportunity to approach total strangers and dredge information out of them with a series of probing questions. Somehow he had to become that person again, even if it was just for a few hours.

As he passed a few family groups and a handful of sun–worshippers, he tried to remember how the old Tyler would have acted. He would have flattered the women with his charming smile and won the confidence of the men with his easy–going personality. He realized he rarely even looked people in the eye anymore; why would he when he didn't really want to have a conversation with anyone?

Before he knew it, he had reached the beach bar he'd heard about. Although it was not yet noon, there was reggae music playing loudly and a few people sat at the bar and surrounding tables. He decided the best place to start would be in the atmosphere he was most comfortable in.

"One Heineken, please," he said to the bartender. Slipping onto one of the high stools, he turned his body at an angle so that he could appreciate the view. The building was completely open on the sea side and it was hard to ignore the picture–perfect scene of blue–green waters framed by palm trees and sand.

"Is there a place down here called Sunny Island Primary School?" he asked the bartender when he returned.

"Yes, but it's not open on Sunday. You will have to wait until tomorrow to enroll," the man replied with a laugh.

Tyler chuckled obligingly. "Ever heard of a woman named Lucy Brookstone who had something to do with that school?"

"Lucy?" The bartender shook his head thoughtfully. "Don't think I know anybody with that name, but you never can be sure. You should ask Ingrid, she is the teacher over there."

"Ingrid. Where can I find Ingrid?"

"She live up on the hill but you can find her down here in a few hours. She always comes down to hear the music on Sunday afternoon. She love to dance, that one."

Okay, he was making progress. He paid for his beer and carried it with him down the beach a short way. He sat under a stand of manchioneal trees and watched several children splashing in a shallow pool. Formed by a coral reef that ran for several hundred yards about ten feet from shore, this safe place to swim was apparently one of the main attractions of Lower Bay.

Nearby a young local man was digging in the sand with a very white boy and girl. The children clearly adored his attention, as he alternated his sandcastle building with handstands and bellyflops in the water and other various high jinks. Their mother sat nearby with a bottle of SPF 45 suntan lotion close at hand.

"Can Calvin come home with us for lunch? Can he? Can he?" they pleaded with her.

For the next half hour Tyler watched Calvin greet nearly everyone on the beach as they passed by. Tourists and locals alike seemed to know the muscular young male who wore only a pair of bright yellow shorts and a big grin on his dark face. Tyler decided that if anybody was his man, Calvin was. He would know who had come and gone in Lower Bay over the last few months and he would definitely know the children.

After a while Calvin became aware of the fact that Tyler had been looking at him and used the opportunity to bum a cigarette. "Sorry, I don't smoke," Tyler apologized, wondering why he felt had to apologize for not smoking.

"That's all right, you can buy me a beer instead," Calvin laughed and then quickly put up a hand. "Just joking, mon, only if you want to."

"No, I will, definitely. But since you seem to know everybody, I want to ask you a few questions. I'm Tyler Mackenzie, by the way," he held out his hand.

"Mackenzie." Calvin repeated the name, tipping his head quizzically for a brief second. "I'm Calvin. You want to walk over to the bar?"

Tyler shouldered his pack and they began to walk together in the direction of the beach restaurant, which was now quite full. The children clamored after them until Calvin gave his assurance that he would be back in a few minutes.

"You have some family that ever live on this island?" Calvin asked him. "I knew some people named Mackenzie here a little while ago."

"Not that I know of." Tyler elbowed his way into the bar and came back with two beers. "Let's sit out on the beach where we can talk."

They settled themselves and their cold beers a short distance away in the shade. "So are you from Lower Bay, Calvin?" Tyler asked.

"Yes, mon. Born and raised right on de hillside behind de village well. You been down dat way yet?" Calvin gave a nod of his head in a easterly direction behind them. "I will show you later if you like. "

"How is it all the tourists know you?"

Calvin shrugged and gave a dazzling grin. "I am just a friendly guy, plays with their children, maybe they buy me lunch, maybe they give me a ticket to the States. Who knows?"

"Ever meet a lady named Lucy Brookstone?'

"What she look like?"

"About this tall, long wavy copper–colored hair, lots of freckles. Had a little boy."

Calvin's eyes narrowed as he gave Tyler a long, hard quizzical look. "No," he answered finally. "I never meet anybody I remember with that name. Why you looking for her? She a girlfriend of yours?"

"Once upon time. Actually I am looking for her son, not her. According to the London Times she died in a car crash a few months ago. You know of any little white boys without mothers on this island?"

Calvin shook his head and took a long swallow of beer before replying. "Why you come to Lower Bay asking questions like that, mon? We are a quiet place, no big TV kind of crime going on here." But for some reason, he seemed agitated so Tyler pressed on.

"You know the Sunny Island Primary School?"

"I should know it. My sister is de second teacher there." Calvin laughed. "It a nice little school just across de way from here. Why you asking?"

Tyler retrieved the now dog–eared Fed Ex envelope from his pack and pointed out the line in the obituary. "You see she asked to have contributions sent there. She must know it somehow."

He could see Calvin mouthing the words to himself as he slowly read the end of the paragraph. Visual aids might be more helpful in this case.

"Here, let me show you this picture. Maybe you will remember having seen her on the beach or some place. Or maybe we can show it to your sister."

As he stared at the photograph, Calvin's body became perfectly still, like an animal in the wild who has just spotted his prey. "Dis woman? And dis is de boy you are looking for?"

Tyler's heart raced with excitement. "You know them?"

Calvin looked away and out to sea where four young boys were shouting and splashing as they all tried to ride a single surfboard. "I have seen some whose likeness favor dem," he replied. "But de woman have short curly hair, very white blonde and de boy is much older. And her name it not Lucy....what you say?"

"Brookstone."

"No, her name was not Lucy Brookstone." Calvin turned back to Tyler now with a steely gaze that pierced through his merry demeanor. "Her name was Ruby."

"Ruby?"

"Yes, Ruby. Ruby Mackenzie, like your name be." Calvin finished his beer in another long gulp and slammed it down into the sand. "Now you tell me who is bullshitting who here, Mr. Tyler Mackenzie."

"What?" Tyler felt like all the air had been compressed out of his lungs. "Wait!" he shouted after Calvin who was retreating angrily down the beach. "What about the boy? What was his name?"

"She call him 'T', like the letter. That all anybody know him as. Now don' ax me anymore. I know your kind." Calvin moved quickly through the manchioneal trees that lined the edge of the beach and took off at a jog down the road.

Tyler sat dumbfounded, staring after him, trying to comprehend what had just taken place. Calvin had identified Lucy as someone named Ruby Mackenzie and for some reason had gotten pissed off at him because of it. Even though he couldn't fathom why, it didn't matter at this point. Calvin had just given him the most important piece of information so far. Even if he didn't know what the hell to do with it.

When he heard the band begin to play, he went back up to De Reef. The place was filled with people now, sitting at the tables, three deep at the bar and spilling out onto the beach. It was hard to believe there were so many people on this little island. Judging from the yachts moored in the bay, some of the Sunday guests were visitors from other places as well.

He managed to elbow his way through the crowd and finally caught the eye of the bartender who had waited on him before. "Ingrid here yet?" he asked after ordering another beer. The bartender pointed to a tall woman standing at the edge of the area designated as a dance floor. Tyler moved away from the bar and leaned on a post to study her.

Ingrid had a classic Nordic physique, big–boned and long–limbed, with the large muscular thighs of a runner or hiker, and an equally Nordic face with high, sculpted cheekbones and full lips. Her dark hair was cropped short in a very European style and had a few well–placed gold streaks in it. She wore short blue shorts and an orange bikini top, both of which showed off her well–rounded feminine assets to their fullest as she tapped her foot and swayed her wide hips to the beat of the music, seemingly impatient for a song she could dance to.

Standing there with a glass of wine in one hand and a cigarette in the other, she was far from his traditional image of a schoolteacher but she fit right into the laid–back scene of Lower Bay. Someone at a table nearby called something out to her and when she threw back her head and laughed, she had a dazzling smile. Her self–assuredness made Tyler feel more insecure than he might have expected. At one time, he would have welcomed any opportunity to approach a woman like Ingrid. Now it took an enormous amount of courage to even consider it.

When the band launched into a Bob Marley set, Ingrid put down her drink and tapped another woman on the shoulder. Her friend was a stunning black woman wearing a tight–fitting tank top and a long gauzy skirt. Her outfit displayed her full–breasted figure, narrow waist and muscular arms while gracefully concealing the larger dimensions of the lower half of her body. As the two of them gyrated in a sensual and uninhibited way to the syncopated beat of the music, all eyes in the bar watched their movements. This was definitely not the time to approach Ingrid for a discreet conversation.

Other dancers joined them, but none seemed to enjoy themselves to the same extent as the schoolteacher and her friend. When the band finally took a break, Ingrid, drenched with sweat, moved rapidly to the bar to request a bottle of water. Tyler sensed his opportunity and crossed quickly to join her, getting her attention as he bumped against her wet arm to place his empty on the bar.

The manner in which she gave him the once—over told him volumes about her. "You're Ingrid, right?"

"I am. And you are..."

"Tyler. I was wondering if I could talk to you." To his own ears, he sounded stupid, like a teenager.

Ingrid gave him a crooked grin. "I'm sure you could do more than talk to me if I gave you the chance." she upended the water bottle into her mouth, wiped the back of her hand across her lips and gazed at him frankly.

Her direct come—on made him flush in surprise. "What would your boyfriend say to that?" he managed to sputter out.

She shook her head. "It's not as simple as that." He could hear her slight Swedish accent now. "I'm in love with someone who doesn't love me back." She sighed. "So where are you from?"

"Most recently, Grenada." Tyler realized she thought he was just another guy trying to pick her up, something she seemed to be quite comfortable with. "Look, let's get a couple of drinks and then go somewhere that we can talk."

Her response was to take his hand off the empty bottle he was clutching and lead him towards the door. "There's a much quieter little bar just at the bend in the road," she said. "We can get something there."

The road was hot and dusty in the late afternoon sun. The loud conversation and music faded to the distant beat of an insistent bass line as they headed into the cluster of houses that comprised the local village. As they passed the village well, which was an old—fashioned hand pump mounted on a stone base, a couple of local men hailed Ingrid cheerfully. "Is that where you get your water?" Tyler asked curiously.

"No, only the very poorest people still use the well. The rest of us have cisterns under our houses." She pointed up a dirt road. "Up there is the school where I teach."

"The Sunny Islands Primary School."

"You know it already?" Before he could reply, she said, "Here we are," and waved her hand at a colorful little establishment across the way. They ordered a couple of drinks, Mt. Gay with lime for him and a white wine for her, and then sat at a white resin table on the tiny veranda.

"Now. What did you want to talk to me about? I was born in Stockholm thirty–one years ago, grew up in a little town in the north of Sweden, went to university at Goteburg and taught school in a tiny village in Lapland for a year and a half year before I came here on a vacation with my boyfriend. He went home, I stayed and the rest, as you Americans say, is history," Ingrid peered at him mischievously over the rim of her glass and rubbed the bare skin on the top of his foot with her big toe. "What more do you need to know?"

Tyler abruptly pulled his foot away and cleared his throat. "Actually I wanted to talk to you about the school. Did you ever know anybody named Lucy Brookstone who was connected to the school in some way?"

Ingrid's forehead furrowed into a little frown. "No, I don't think so…"

"Okay, how about this then." He showed her the photograph of Lucy and Tucker. "Ever meet this woman or this boy?"

There was a faint whooshing sound, as Ingrid softly sucked in her breath. "Where did you get this?"

"I take it you know her."

"I might have known her once. And her name is?"

"Lucy Brookstone." He watched her eyes widen. "But maybe you knew her as Ruby Mackenzie."

Ingrid sat back in her chair and sipped her drink, regaining her composure. "Maybe I did."

"How recently?"

Ingrid shrugged. "I have no idea. What are you, a cop or something?"

Tyler grinned a bit grimly. "I guess I'm an 'or something'. I used to be an investigative journalist. Same as Lucy. Whom you knew as Ruby. "

"Must not be the same person then. The Ruby I knew was nothing of the kind." She downed her glass of wine and Tyler signaled the bartender for another round. He wasn't going to let her get away that easily.

"What did Ruby do here?"

"Let me ask you a question, Mr. Tyler." Ingrid met his gaze for a minute and held it. "Why are you looking for this person named Lucy?"

For an answer, Tyler handed her the obituary. At first Ingrid looked startled and then she threw back her head and laughed. "This is total bullshit."

"How so?"

Because it never happened. At least not here. And especially not the funeral part." She pointed a derogatory finger at the article.

"Why is that?"

"Because nobody gets cremated here. Her ashes couldn't have been spread at sea."

Tyler sat in stunned silence for a moment, impressed with Ingrid's reasoning. "So what do you think happened then?"

"What do you mean?"

"Where is Lucy–Ruby then? She and her son seem to have disappeared."

Ingrid gratefully accepted her next drink before replying. "I can honestly say that I don't have a clue where Ruby is."

"And what else can you honestly tell me?"

"That you're the most interesting man I've met in months." And this time her big toe traced the curve of his calf up to the back of his knee.

Tyler didn't want to be Ingrid's most interesting man. He wanted to find out what happened to Lucy. But he sensed that maybe the two went hand in hand.

Matching Tyler drink for drink, it did not take long before Ingrid began to get pretty sloppy. Tyler thought it might be a good opportunity to bring up Lucy again.

"Did Ruby's son go to your school?"

"Ruby's son. What was his name? Maybe he did." Ingrid stood up suddenly and staggered sideways. Tyler leaped to his feet and steadied her at the elbow.

"Tucker. I think he might have been known as T. Maybe I should walk you home," he suggested.

"I definitely think you should take me home." Ingrid giggled and stared out to sea where the reflection of the setting sun was dancing on top of the waves.

He paid the bill and discreetly asked the bartender how far away Ingrid lived. "Just up de road. Not far. A colorful house with a big veranda."

"So Ruby's son, T. Did he go to your school?"

"T. What kind of name is that? I would remember a boy with a name like a letter of the alphabet." She giggled again.

Even drunk, she was really good at this game. For some reason she was protecting Lucy, which meant she knew a lot more than she was letting on.

"She was Kip Kingsley's girlfriend. Did you know that about her?" He slipped his arm through hers and led her out into the road.

"Who, Ruby? You're shitting me, right?"

"Shitting you? What kind of way is that for a schoolteacher to talk?"

"You're telling me that Ruby was Kip Kingsley's girlfriend?" Well, at least she was admitting that she knew Ruby.

"That's right. She left me for him. Can you imagine – she gave up a one bedroom flat with a struggling journalist to shack up with a millionaire has–been rocker with a penthouse in London."

"I hear he has a house on Mustique." She nodded her head in a southerly direction and then lurched a little that same way.

Tyler had temporarily forgotten this important detail. "How far is Mustique from here?"

"I don't know, maybe ten or twenty miles. You can see it from Paget Farm or by the airport. "Ingrid turned suddenly onto a dirt path that led up a steep hill. "Short cut," she explained.

"Is there a ferry that goes to Mustique?" he asked.

"Ha. No, Mustique is very private. Even the mail boat doesn't stop there. You could charter a boat or a plane. Or you can fly there from St. Vincent. Why – are you thinking of visiting Kip Kingsley? If you do, then please take me with you, please! It would be so awesome to meet him."

Tyler could not understand what power the man seemed to have over women. He decided it was time he joined in Ingrid's game. "But then he might become the most interesting man you've met in months."

Ingrid turned to him as her foot touched the bottom step of a set of steep turquoise stairs. "But I haven't met him yet," she said, covering his lips with her own.

As they sank down on the steps, he realized that as strange as the afternoon had been, he felt more like his old self than he had in five long years.

CHAPTER FIVE

The explosion rocked him backward and then he saw the car engulfed in flames. With sudden horror, he realized that Lucy and Tucker were trapped inside and he was the only one who knew. He had to save them but the fire was so hot and he couldn't get to the car...

Tyler jerked awake and sat up, dripping with sweat. The same old nightmare but with a new variation this time, adding Lucy and Tucker to the picture. Instead of being free of his past, it was not only coming back to haunt him full force, it was twisting itself into the present.

He looked around in the semi–darkness, trying to remember where he was. The shapes in the room, the windows, even the silhouette of the body next to him were not familiar. He felt momentary panic at being out of touch with time and place, before it all came back to him.

Ingrid's house. That's where he was. Ingrid's colorful cottage in Lower Bay in the middle of the night. He couldn't leave now if he wanted to. He had no idea how to get back to his hotel in the harbor; he had come by water taxi so he had never even traversed the distance on land.

He remembered following her across a spacious, airy living room, she undressing as she walked, tossing the bikini top onto a chair and leaving the shorts on the floor where she stepped out of them. He tried to take in the surroundings, the bright hibiscus print cushions of the couch and chairs, the mosaic work along the kitchen counter, but she pulled him along after her into a bedroom lined with windows that overlooked the valley and the sea.

When she left the door open, he'd asked her if she lived alone.

"No, I have a roommate, but she is away in Barbados for a few days." She reached for his shirt and pulled it over his head.

For falling into bed with a near stranger, it had been damn good sex. Ingrid was totally uninhibited and not afraid to express her enjoyment. Tyler had a feeling the whole village must have known when she reached orgasm, but she didn't seem to care. Afterwards they had both fallen sound asleep without even speaking.

His stomach grumbled and Tyler realized he could not remember the last time he'd eaten. Slipping out of bed, he moved quietly into the living room, letting his eyes adjust to the darkness. Finally he could make out the shape of a refrigerator in the kitchen area and was relieved when its interior light showed him not only its contents but illuminated a switchplate on the wall as well.

Munching on a cold chicken leg, he studied the notices and flyers under the palm tree magnets on the refrigerator door. He immediately zeroed in on a large handmade birthday card to Ingrid signed by all the kids in the school. He was not surprised to see a big "T" among the names, but the chicken bone stopped halfway to his mouth when he saw the cursive scrawl that formed "Ruby" at the bottom of the page.

Apparently Ingrid knew Ruby a lot better than she was letting on. He read everything on the refrigerator, but found nothing else very intriguing.

Looking around the dimly lit room, he realized the most valuable asset to his investigation in the house was Ingrid. And if she wanted to use him to relieve her horniness, then he should have no guilt about using her the way he wanted to. It could be a mutually beneficial relationship, with no strings attached, of course.

As he wandered back into the bedroom, he went over in his mind what he had learned in the last two days. There had been no car accident, Lucy had spent some unspecified amount of time here under the name of Ruby Mackenzie, and for some reason both Calvin and Ingrid were protecting her. And, to top off the strange information he had learned, nobody was ever cremated on Bequia.

So if all signs pointed to Lucy still being alive, would Amelia want him to continue his search? Well, until he could prove conclusively that she wasn't dead, the answer was most likely an unequivocal yes.

Sliding under the top sheet, he ran a finger slowly down the length of Ingrid's back until his hand came to rest in the warm moistness between her legs. She stirred and rolled towards him with a contented sigh of anticipation.

The next time he opened his eyes, Ingrid was gone and sunlight streamed through the open windows. The smell of coffee brewing was nearly as arousing as the sex had been. Through the open doorway he could see Ingrid in the kitchen, her dark hair wet and glistening, a green sarong knotted around her torso just above her breasts.

He knew more about the secret crevices of her body than he did about who she was.

Sensing his eyes on her, she turned, her full lips expanding into a grin. "Good morning, lover," she said. "Want some coffee?" Without waiting for a reply, she poured two mugs. "How do you like it?"

"Just milk, thanks."

She sat on the edge of the bed, still smiling but looking at him intently. "Okay, I am embarrassed to admit this," she began and true enough, her cheeks were tinged with pink, "but I can't remember your name."

Tyler laughed heartily. "Do you remember anything we talked about yesterday?"

"Yes," she replied defensively. "Everything but your name." She patted his bare leg beneath the sheet.

"So if you have such a good memory, tell me what else you remember about Ruby Mackenzie."

Without replying, she stood up abruptly and slid open the mirrored closet door. "I have to get ready for work," was all she said. Untying the sarong and letting it fall to the floor, she stood there stark naked gazing at the clothes on the hangers.

"You don't want to come back to bed for a little while?"

"Can't. I'll be late for school. But you're welcome to stay as long as you like." She pulled on a pair of purple bikini underpants and chose a batik sundress with a pattern of fish on it.

"How about if I come back and take you to dinner tonight?"

She stopped dressing momentarily to stare at him. "Okay," she said finally. "Make a reservation at Fernando's and be here by seven."

He wasn't sure if she would respond better if he acted casual or seductive. Leaning back against the pillow, he tried his best imitation of both. "Sounds good. How about I come at six for...cocktails?"

She raised one eyebrow and gave him a reproving look. "I am a schoolteacher, you know," she teased.

"Well, maybe that will give us time for you to teach me a thing or two before dinner. Oh, and by the way, my name is Tyler."

She blushed again. "Why was I thinking it was Kip?"

Tyler laughed. "Maybe because you got all excited when I mentioned that my friend Lucy, aka Ruby, used to be Kip Kingsley's girlfriend."

Enlightenment dawned in her eyes. "Oh, I'd forgotten that part of our conversation. He's come here a few times, you know." Turning her back to him, she rummaged through a wicker basket of jewelry.

"Kip Kingsley has?" The light bantering tone was gone from his voice now.

"Yeah, he played during the jazz festival last year and then showed up at De Reef one Sunday afternoon. He and that guy who's the leader singer from that Irish band...what's it called? Apoplexica? Can't remember his name, but I remember seeing the two of them at the bar with a couple of women in bikinis..."

Her words faded away into the hissing sound that filled Tyler's head. Apoplexica. It was a name he had not allowed himself to utter or even think for the last five years. A name that could seriously unlock the floodgates of terror and emotion that he had tried not to drown in. How was it possible that a single phone call could trigger a new series of events that might bring everything back that he had run away from?

"Tyler? Are you all right? I've got to go now."

He blinked. Ingrid was waving her hand back and forth in front of his face and giggling.

"I'm fine. I – I just think I need a little more sleep." What he really wanted to do was pull the sheet up over his head and disappear back into his non–existence on Grenada.

"Okay. See you tonight then." She gave him a kiss that was ripe with promise and left the room.

Apoplexica. It was just the name of a band. The lead singer had been here once, she'd said. It was just a coincidence. No big deal.

Sinking down into the mattress, he hid his head under a pillow to shut out the daylight. But as he started to drift off, he shook himself awake. If he fell asleep, he knew the dreams would bring it all back, just like they had been doing for the last two days. He could lose his past easier in the reality of the present.

Leaping out of bed, he headed for the bathroom to take a shower. When he emerged from the steamy stall ten minutes later, the only towel he could find was a hand towel. Drying off the best he could with it, he hung it back on the rack and stepped out into the living room to air–dry the rest of the water on his body.

"Oh sorry I didn't know anybody was here," he heard a male voice exclaim and then, "What the fuck? What are you doing here?"

He turned around to see Calvin holding a loaf of bread in one hand and brandishing a long serrated knife in the other. Tyler swallowed hard and backed towards the bedroom door. "Hey, how you doing, Calvin. Guess I could ask you the same question."

"You're not welcome in this house, Mr. Investigator," Calvin snarled.

"I think Ingrid might disagree with you," Tyler called over his shoulder as he quickly slipped his shorts on. "You're not the roommate, are you?"

"My sister lives here. And sometimes so do I. And if I had been here last night, you wouldn't have reach the front door, never mind the bed. You lazy bumba clot, making de lady drunk and crazy and den fucking her to fin' out what you want fah know–"

"Hold on a second there." Tyler cut short Calvin's tirade of patois. "You must know as well as I do that Ingrid had a lot to do with bringing me through that door and into the bed. My guess is I'm not the first guy you've found here in the morning without his pants on."

Calvin tried to maintain his scowling expression but could not keep the corners of his mouth from turning up slightly. "Okay, mon, you are right. Ingrid can get so hot sometime you think she might burn you like one sizzling fry pan. What she tell you?"

"About Lucy? I mean, Ruby?" Tyler did not wait for his reply. "Well, she told me quite a lot. You mean about, uh, Ruby and the school and about Kip Kingsley coming here–"

"You can't fool me, mon. Ingrid not foo–foo. She not tell you nothing. You got you one nice piece of Swedish ass, now you can go leave us be." Calvin turned his back on Tyler while he opened a jar of guava jelly, signaling that the conversation was over.

Retreating to the bedroom, Tyler finished dressing and collected his things. He needed to win these villagers over one way or another. They clearly knew more than they were letting on.

"Calvin, if you want to earn some money, I could really use some local help with this investigation I'm working on."

For an answer, Calvin smacked the jelly down onto his bread with the kind of force West Indians use when they slap dominoes onto a table. Then, taking a large bite of his breakfast, he glared lethally at Tyler.

"Okay, well, think about it. I'm hoping you'll change your mind. See you later."

Stepping out onto the deck, he took in the breathtaking view of Lower Bay that he had been too preoccupied to see the night before. The blinding brightness of the morning sun gave a clarity to the colors and shapes of the landscape around him that seemed fresh. Or maybe it was just the state of his mind. Like an old pair of unused scissors, it was getting looser and easier the more he worked it, not cutting as perfectly as it once did, but with a little sharpening it might soon be in working order again.

He found his way back down to the main road through the village and then stopped to ask an old woman sweeping her yard how to get back to the harbor. "Walk up to the top and catch the dollar bus," she replied waving her hand up to where the road wound steeply up towards the hills. "Or if you not have a dollar, you can go in by foot. I see many of your kind who do so."

He did not know what his kind was, but he assumed she meant white tourists who wanted exercise and were probably too frightened of local culture to squeeze into a crowded minibus with strangers of a different skin color. It was a picturesque climb, with hairpin turns and steep drop–offs, but by the time he reached the junction of the village road with the main island road, he was hot and sweaty and ready not just for a ride but maybe a drink as well.

The dollar bus dropped him in the center of town where local vendors were setting up their stands for the day. Fresh bread, neat stacks of limes, baskets of tomatoes and bananas, boxes of green beans and christophines and callaloo. He bypassed all of these choices for an ice cold Hairoun beer at an upstairs internet café with a view of the harbor, hating himself for his addiction but needing to satisfy it at the same time.

He might as well start his day's work by sending an email to Amelia. It had been weeks since he'd last checked his email, so it was no surprise that the inbox was full and unable to receive any more messages. Daunted by the task of reading old communications from friends and family as well as sorting out the junk mail and spam, he considered just blowing the whole thing off, getting on the next ferry to St. Vincent and then catching the next plane to Grenada. He could be home in a few hours, back to his world of rum–soaked numbness. It would be so much easier and so much safer than going on with finding out what had happened to Lucy.

He stared out at the sailboats in the bay and thought over the events of the last day as he finished the beer. Well, if nothing else, he should at least let Amelia know the obituary was false. She was paying him to do a job for her and even if he had no responsibility to his own expectations, he still didn't like to let other people down.

Turning back to the computer, he deleted all but a few of the outdated unread messages, which he saved for another time. But at least now there was room for any new ones that might come in.

Even though it was a small step, the significance of it scared him. To balance things out, he ordered another beer before starting his email to Amelia.

By midday Tyler was back in Lower Bay, sitting at the bar at De Reef. He realized the only way he was going to find out anything about Lucy/Ruby was in the village where she apparently had spent the last few years of her life. There had to be someone who knew her who would talk. He just had to keep trying.

Moses, the bartender, had been working the previous day and he immediately remembered Tyler. "Dat Ingrid, she a nice lady, yeah?" he asked. Probably half the village knew by now that Tyler had spent the night with her.

"Very nice. We're having dinner tonight at Fernando's." Might as well let him know Ingrid was willing to see him again. "I guess she was pretty close to my friend, Ruby, huh?"

Moses nodded vigorously. "Yes, those two together most of the time, they work together, live together, go out together."

Live together, Tyler mused excitedly. Ingrid and Calvin were sitting on much more than he had realized. "I guess that must have been before – uh, what's the name of the other woman who lives up there again?"

"Justine. You meet her?" Moses glanced towards the beach where two elderly women in skirted swimsuits and bathing caps were making their way up the sand towards the restaurant. He started mixing up a couple of gin and tonics, so Tyler figured the old ladies must be regulars.

"No, she's away right now. Calvin's sister, right?"

"Not just his sister, mon. Twin sister. But Justine get sent away as a little girl because Calvin's mama already have five children before the twins whom she cannot feed. Justine get adopted by a family on St. Thomas and nobody see her again until she grown."

"That's kind of sad," Tyler commented. "This seems like a nice place to grow up."

"Not with seven in one room and not enough to eat. Justine is the lucky one. She got a good education and went to art school. Calvin have to scrape by here at home. Excuse me." Moses carried the drinks he had made to a table that faced the sea and then pulled out the chairs to accommodate the two women who had finally made it up the steps. "Ladies, good afternoon. Your drinks are ready."

"Oh, Moses, you are so good to us. Isn't he a dear, Liz?"

While Moses was busy taking their order, Tyler turned his attention to the occupants of the barstools on either side of him. To his right, two taxi drivers were having a heated discussion about the outcome of a local cricket match. On his left, a young couple whispered German endearments while caressing each other's suntanned thighs. Nobody else seemed likely to know anything that might have any bearing on what had happened to Lucy.

He sipped his beer slowly, waiting for Moses to have time for another chat. When the bartender finally approached him again, Tyler asked him about Kip Kingsley. "I hear he comes here sometimes," he said with what he hoped was the tone of an excited fan.

"Yes, he has come a couple of times lately. After he play the music festival. He have a house on Mustique, they say."

"So like when was he last here?"

Moses scratched his chin. "Maybe a month, maybe two. Not long. That time he come with his friend from another band. Ritchie!" He called loudly to one of the taxi drivers. "What the name of de band de guy come from, de one here with Kingsley last time?"

"Uh... what they call themselves....Apple something."

Apoplexica again. He did not want to know they had been here on this island, maybe sat at this same place at the bar. He did not want them to have anything in common with him; not with Lucy or Ruby or even Bequia.

"Yeah, anyway, him with dis heavy metal man famous over England way. Come on one fancy big yacht, everybody get so drunk they have to stay the night out there in the bay and sail back to Mustique in the morning. They spend a lot of money in dis bar, mon. A lot of money." Moses shook his head. "Someday I like to know what it like to have money like dat man have."

"You will never know dat, Moses, less you leave dat big idea wife of yours!" Ritchie laughed at him and then the three local men began speaking a very fast local patois as they made jokes about Moses and his wife.

Tyler bought another beer and wandered onto the beach. Stretching out in the shade of the manchioneal trees near the shallow reef pool, he wondered if there was any connection between Kip's last visit to Bequia and Lucy's disappearance. Maybe the answer was simple – maybe she and Tucker had gone back to Mustique with him.

But that didn't explain the fake obituary or the strange behavior of her friends. Unless Kip had sent it to the paper and Ingrid and Calvin were in on it with him.

It was too much to contemplate and the afternoon heat was making him very sleepy.

The man in black was sprinting down the street, looking over his shoulder every few seconds as he ran. When he turned the corner Tyler could no longer see him from the window of his third floor flat but there was something about the man's behavior that was familiar and disturbing. Without knowing exactly what compelled him, he ran down the three flights of stairs and flew out of the front door onto the street. It was a crisp, sunny afternoon and he could see a woman and her child on the sidewalk, enjoying the day—

"Tyler Mackenzie. Mr. Investigator. What's ,happening?"

Perspiration dripping from his brow, Tyler sat up breathing hard. Calvin stood over him, looking puzzled. "Bad dream? You look like you gone have a heart attack, mon."

Tyler put his head between his knees for a second and tried to calm down. If this kept up he would never be able to sleep again. He had to finish this Lucy thing and get back to Grenada. "Yeah, bad dream," he said, looking up at Calvin. "The worst."

Calvin sat down next to him, digging his broad bare feet into the warm sand. "I see you in the bar there earlier, talking to Moses."

Tyler nodded silently, still shaken from his nap.

"And I am guessing you axed him about Ruby."

"You mean Ruby the former housemate of Ingrid and your twin sister? Ruby who used to live with Kip Kingsley —"

"What? De musician is who you talkin' about, right? Him play at de jazz festival dis past year? You tellin' me he was Ruby's boyfren'?"

Tyler nodded. "I visited her once at his place in London a long time ago. In fact that was the last time I ever saw her."

"So he de one she runnin' from when she come here? You are not de one who she was hidin' from?"

Tyler tried not to seem too intrigued by Calvin's last remark. "That's right. So you've known her for a while, then."

"Yes, mon. I have known her since the day she arrive. I know Ruby better than any man on dis island."

Of course, Calvin the self–appointed welcoming committee of Lower Bay would have been the first to accost Ruby and her son. For now, Tyler had to dismiss the rest of the relationship implicit in Calvin's remark.

Tyler stood up and brushed the sand off himself. "Calvin, will you let me buy you a beer? I think I really need your help."

Calvin took Tyler up to a much fancier bar called Coco's perched on the side of a cliff overlooking Lower Bay. It was painted turquoise and pink and purple and because of its colorful Caribbean ambience and breathtaking view, it was a popular place with tourists. The drinks cost twice as much as they should, but Tyler didn't care. In the middle of a Monday afternoon the place was empty and therefore a good place to have a private conversation.

"So if you and Ruby were good friends," he began eagerly, once they were settled at a discreet distance from the female bartender who was watching a soap opera on a large screen TV near the bar, " then you know where she is now? Where she went to?"

Calvin gave him a piercing look and took a swallow of beer. "Why you need to know that?"

"I'm being paid by her sister to find out. Actually to find her son, Tucker. Her sister thinks she's dead. I showed you that obituary. Yesterday, on the beach."

"So how you think that got in that paper? You sure Ruby is the same person as your friend?"

Tyler stirred the ice in his rum and squeezed the slice of lime perched on the rim of the glass. "Now that is a very good question. About the obituary, I mean. I have no idea how or why that got into the paper. But it sure made it easier for Lucy to disappear."

"And she is your relation, right?"

"My relation?"

"Well, you are both Mackenzie." Calvin lifted an eyebrow inquisitively.

"But she's not really Mackenzie. I don't know why she took my last name. Must have been the first thing that popped into her mind when she had to make something up." Tyler's mental wheels were spinning now, trying to piece the story together.

"How do I know you aren't making this whole thing up? Maybe you just want to find her and hurt her like—" Calvin closed his mouth into a tight line, perhaps realizing he'd already said more than he'd intended to.

"Look, here's what I know happened." He did not definitively know anything, but he was going to do his damnedest to act like he did. "Lucy came to Bequia with her little boy to hide from something or someone. To be on the safe side, she changed her name and apparently cut and colored her hair as well. She stayed here for two years quite happily, but then one day Kip shows up on the island to play a concert and then a few months later, he shows up here in Lower Bay. And then Lucy disappears again. An obituary appears in the London Times declaring her dead. So where do we think she is?"

Calvin shook his head. "I honestly can say I don't know, mon. I only hope she not back wit' him."

But what if she was back with Kip on Mustique? A cold sweat broke out on Tyler's brow and his hands began to tremble. He put down his drink. "Calvin, I need your help. If you work on this with me, I can even pay you for your time."

The mention of money had a curious effect on Calvin. Tyler could see the internal battle that went on before Calvin finally answered him in a quiet voice. "You not need to pay me. I want to know Ruby is safe as much as you do. You just need to take care of me, expenses and all."

"Deal." Tyler extended his hand and Calvin gave it a firm, muscular shake.

He suspected that Calvin's real reason in wanting to help him was to keep him from finding out too much, to continue to protect Lucy/Ruby in some way. But at least he had the sense they were on the same side.

"Now here's the first thing I need you to help me do." Tyler downed the rest of his rum in one gulp and paused to enjoy the exhilarating rush of numbness filling his brain. "I need you to tell me how we get to Mustique."

CHAPTER SIX

The steep hills that surrounded the village of Lower Bay were awash in the blushing afterglow of the sunset as Tyler once again climbed the steps to Ingrid's deck. He'd barely had time to return to the Frangipani for an end of the day shower before he was due to show up for "cocktails." Consequently, he'd splurged on a taxi from town, taxi, of course, meaning an open pickup truck that had been outfitted with seats and a canvas roof and sides that could be rolled down in case of rain. It cost fifteen times as much as the dollar bus, but took him right to the door.

He was disappointed to hear voices as he neared the top of the wooden stairs; it meant that he and Ingrid would not be alone and a pre–dinner, sex warm–up might be out of the question. But when he entered the house he saw an unfamiliar backside covered by a brilliant emerald green skirt in a tribal print. It belonged to a woman who was leaning over to insert a CD into a player that was part of an elaborate stereo system. As she straightened up, he became aware of the smooth, dark skin of her bare back, the lines of which were broken only by the neon yellow ties of a halter top, and of a head full of expensively coifed and beaded braids. He hovered as motionless as she did until the beat of the music kicked in and her body began to sway with natural grace to the Caribbean rhythm.

Swinging her hips she turned towards him and stopped short, sucking in her breath with surprise. Tyler found himself matching her for breathlessness – she was twice as striking as from the front as she was from the back. It was not because of her features; they could be considered typical of the island – full cheeks and lips, a wide nose, large dark eyes, and an ample figure. It was the sophisticated and artistic way she had interpreted herself that was so arresting. The strands of chunky beads framing her neck and wrists, the unique freeform gold hoops dangling from her ears and the unusual contours of the teal eye shadow defining the space beneath her carefully plucked eyebrows – these were the characteristics that separated her from the rest.

"Hello? Can I help you?" she asked him in a melodious voice that was barely louder than a breeze.

"I'm– I'm Tyler," he stammered, stunned by his own feelings of inadequacy and unworldliness in her presence. "You must be Justine. The roommate who was away."

Her deer–caught–in–the–headlights pose disappeared and amusement lit up her eyes. He could see the resemblance to Calvin as her face softened into the pleasant lines of a smile. "And you must be the one who spent the night here." She held out a hand highlighted by sparkly fuchsia nails. "Nice to meet you. Ingrid and my brother are out on the deck."

Justine met his gaze for only a second, but that was all it took. He was captured in the net of her exotic mystique, enchanted more by what she hadn't said than by the few words she did. When she left him to go into the kitchen, he was unable to move, tethered to the spot by an invisible strand of the faint perfume that she left behind.

Snatches of the conversation taking place on the porch finally released his bonds and brought him back to reality.

"…never told him she lived here…"

"Me never tell him so!"

"…find out…"

"…investigator. Him know how…"

Tyler inched silently across the painted wooden floor towards the open back door, stopping again just out of view.

"...gets you drunk and foo–foo at Nando's tonight, you never know what you might say."

"Look, don't worry about me, okay. We just try to keep an eye on what he does as much as we can and–"

"Hey no problem, he axe me to be him partner. I be with him ahl day, you can fuck the man senseless ahl night."

"Calvin!" He could hear them both laughing.

"For your sake, I hope him good in bed."

"Not to worry, mon," Ingrid affected a Caribbean accent here, "Him one a de best," and Calvin broke up into loud guffaws.

"Why you not joining them?" Justine's voice at Tyler's shoulder made him twitch with guilt.

He might be a good lay, but he could not think of a good lie. "They were talking about my sexual performance," he replied truthfully with a mischievous grin. "And I wanted to hear what they said."

"Don' tell me, I don' wan' to know!" Justine covered her ears in jest. "There is no privacy in this house, none at all!" She gave him a little shove through the door. "Go on, now. Face the music, boy."

He could come up with a dozen good reasons why he should blow off Ingrid and Calvin and spend the evening getting to know this bewitching woman whose hands had left two hot and tingling spots in the center of his back. But the two on the porch had already spotted him.

"Speakin' of de devil himself–"

"Calvin. Didn't expect to see you here again," Tyler remarked as he sat down in a big wooden armchair that would have been called Adirondack style if it had been back in the States.

"Oh, you can't get away from Calvin that easily." Ingrid reached over to put her hand over his for a warm and meaningful second. "He's almost always here."

"Where do you live, Calvin?" Tyler asked as he looked longingly at whatever the golden–hued drinks were that filled their glasses.

"Would you like a rum punch?" Ingrid asked and then without waiting for an answer, she rose and went into the house.

"I sleep at my mother's house but it not a nice place, you know. I prefer it here." Calvin lowered his voice and leaned towards Tyler. "I think I know how we get to Mustique, mon. I check it out tonight, let you know in the mahning."

"Cool. So have you ever been over to Mustique before?" Tyler could hear Ingrid and Justine sharing a confidential girlfriend–type laugh inside the house. It was hard to keep his interest from straying in their direction.

Calvin shook his head. "No, mon. Not on the island itself, just de waters around it. Mustique one very exclusive place. Lotta rich people live there and the islanders are all related to each other and keep to themselves."

"Ruby never talked about living there?"

"Ruby never talk about she past. How we never know she live wit' Kingsley and have him baby, that we have de son of a famous musician living right here? How Kingsley come right to dis village and not know him wife here..." Calvin clucked his tongue a few times and stared off at the darkening sky in contemplation of the great unknown.

"Here you go, lover boy." Ingrid was back with a frosty glass for Tyler's outstretched hand. "But drink up, because we should be on our way."

"You be having snapper tonight, I saw Nando bringing in the catch himself today," Calvin informed them. As the mix of rum and fruit juices momentarily quenched Tyler's perpetual thirst, he pondered the fact that there seemed to be nothing that happened on this little island that everyone else didn't know about. And it could work to a person's advantage – or not.

Fernando's Hideaway was built on the side of a steep hill that overlooked Lower Bay. The restaurant itself was no more than a large open porch built on the side of a house, but despite the simple decor it had the ambience of a chic boutique eatery. From the tables lit by candles in Easy Bake Whole Wheat Flour bags to the wine list written on a chalkboard nailed to the wall, Fernando's seemed to be a secret treasure that returning visitors and expatriate islanders could not get enough of.

A villager himself, Fernando had been a cook on cruise ships for many years before returning home to open a modest bakery and restaurant that employed his sisters as waitresses and other relatives as needed. From his white chef's hat to his trademark bare feet, Fernando's tall frame and lean limbs could be seen in the connecting kitchen as he leaned over the ovens, peering through reading glasses at the roasted potatoes and christophines au gratin.

Ingrid explained all of this to Tyler as they sat at a tiny table for two at the edge of the porch, looking out over the broad moonlit leaves of breadfruit trees growing precariously on the craggy hillside below. More than once, he found himself getting swept up in the romance of the moment, wanting to pretend that he and Ingrid were just what they looked like to anyone who didn't know them – a couple on vacation from their normal life in Elgin, Illinois or Youngstown, Ohio, rekindling their primal passion on a warm night in the tropics.

Instead he said, "So why have you been pretending that you didn't even know Ruby when really she was not only your co–worker but your roommate as well?"

Flushed with surprise by the sudden change in topic, Ingrid sipped her wine for a moment before answering. "Ruby was my friend," she finally replied. "And I don't break promises to friends."

"How did you meet her? Can you tell me that without breaking any promises?" He reached across the table and stroked the soft skin on the inside of her forearm.

Ingrid closed her eyes, partially from the sensation of his touch but also because she appeared to be lost in memory. "Calvin brought her home from the beach one day. Said she needed a place to live for a while and that she could pay half the rent. Justine had gone to New York City for six months and I was struggling to make ends meet." A pained look flashed across her face and, with what seemed to be an almost involuntary gesture, she pulled her arm away from Tyler and rested it in her lap.

"It was a difficult time for me and Ruby was a warm, loving person who helped me as much as I helped her. She wanted to send Tee to preschool but she was funny about him. Didn't let him out of her sight much. And that was how she ended up working with me." Ingrid refilled their glasses from the wine bottle on the table. She seemed intent in thought, studying her drink, and Tyler took the opportunity to watch her face closely.

"Did she ever tell you that you she used to be a journalist? That she wrote investigative exposes for some of the best publications in England?"

"Really? You sure we're talking about the same person here?" She looked up for a second, amused.

"Well, she did change quite a bit over the years, especially after she got together with Kip." Tyler had a fleeting memory of Ruby/Lucy in a bed covered with sheets printed in a musical score.

"So you were her lover before that?" Ingrid's lips curled into an odd half–grin.

"What's so funny about that?"

"It's just interesting to me that we've both slept with you. Maybe someday she and I can compare notes," she teased him, licking the rim of her glass.

"Maybe if you tell me where she went to, you can compare them sooner than someday," he answered, feeling his face flush despite his best efforts.

"Even if I did know, why would I tell you? I barely know you."

Her words gave Tyler a sudden insight into the absurdity of their relationship. It was nothing more than the intimacy of strangers whose paths had crossed because of twisted strokes of fate.

He was saved from having to reply by the arrival of their dinners. The silence surrounding the pleasure of excellent food gave them another sort of intimacy shared by diners in good restaurants everywhere.

Ingrid stopped eating suddenly and began to gesture in the air with a forkful of callaloo. "Ethan Sands," she said suddenly. "That's the name of the guy from Apoplexica that was here at De Reef with Kip Kingsley."

Tyler felt as though the cold wind of a nor'easter was bearing down upon him, sending a chill from his ears to his ankles.

"I guess you're wondering what made me think of that." Ingrid giggled at the strange look on his face. "I heard today that he bought a big house over on Friendship Bay and he's fixing it up so the band can use it as a studio and retreat. How cool is that, huh? Apoplexica here on Bequia. Bet we'll be seeing a lot more musical celebrities once they settle in."

The food on his plate began to spin like a kaleidoscope of shifting tropical shapes and colors. How could this be happening? How had he been seduced out of his safe world on Grenada back into the dark shadows of the life he had left behind? Right now he wanted nothing more than to retreat into a bottle of rum and make it all go away.

"Tyler, are you okay? You look a bit sick."

"I – I – I – Just a little dizziness that's all." He put a hand over his eyes and took a deep breath. "An old head injury, I never know when it's going to act up. I'll be all right in a minute."

"Are you sure? Because we can get this food to go if you want." Ingrid's voice was full of concern that he didn't deserve.

"No, I'm okay." Finding inner strength from some place inside that he hadn't seen in years, he forced himself to pick up his fork and spear a piece of fish.

He would get through the night, he would even enjoy himself, and then in the morning he would leave. Wherever Lucy and Tucker were in the world right now, they would be okay without him finding them.

The decision to go home the next day helped Tyler get through the rest of the meal in a seemingly normal mood. He kept the conversation focused on Ingrid and her own life and by the time they headed back down the hill with full stomachs, they were safely entrenched in the story of her sailing days before she arrived on Bequia.

"Do you know what 'dead reckoning' is?" she asked him as they turned the corner onto the main road that followed the edge of the beach along the moonlit sea.

"It's a sailing term, isn't it?"

"It's how you determine where you're going by calculating it from where you have been. Navigating without the stars and basically without instruments, what you would do in a fog. It's what we had to do one night in a storm off the Canary Islands. The clouds were so thick..."

Tyler didn't hear the rest of what she said. He was trying to figure out if he could apply the concept of dead reckoning to his own life. If he was going to determine where he was headed from where he had been in the last few years it was definitely back to Grenada, where he had absolutely been navigating in a fog. But if he looked at the course of his entire life, Grenada was just a side trip to the doldrums, a disappearance into the Bermuda Triangle, a –

"Yo, Tyler, mon." His thoughts were interrupted by Calvin's voice coming out of the dark behind them.

"Calvin. Where'd you come from?" Tyler twitched a little as Calvin came between them and clapped one large strong hand around each of their shoulders.

"Just been waiting here by de road to see you walking back from Nando's so I could tell you de news."

"The news?"

"I've got a boat to get us to Mustique. Tomorrow. Fast work, don't you know?" Calvin sounded like he was beaming with pleasure.

"Tomorrow? But–"

"Calvin, you de mon!" Ingrid laughed, slapping hands with him in a high five. "Nothing on Bequia you can't manage."

"So, Tyler , we need to be over by Paget Farm at nine, so make sure Ingrid she wake you before she leave for school." Calvin turned away with a sucking sound and Tyler realized he had been carrying a lit joint from which he was now taking a hit.

"Calvin, this is great work, but I hadn't really figured out a plan yet for what we were going to do when we got there." Tyler was backpedalling now, wishing there was a way to put it off a day so he could escape the island and forget the whole affair.

"No problem, we figure something out when we get there. We can always go back. This guy not want much money and him happy to take us any day we want." Calvin held out the smoking spliff to him. "You want some of this?"

After a brief second, Tyler accepted his offering, grateful for any form of escape from his current reality.

Just as he reached the bottom of the stairs, he heard the phone begin to ring. Taking the steps two at a time, he unlocked the door of the flat and leaped towards the phone on the kitchen counter. "Hello? Hello?" But he was too late – the connection had gone dead. He waited for a moment to see if the caller would try again, thinking how odd it was that they hadn't waited for the answering machine to come on.

Seconds later the explosion on the street below rattled the window panes and shook the walls of the building. He raced back to the ground floor and could see the flames through the outside door as soon as he was in the hall. Suddenly he felt as though the slow motion button had been activated and his arms and legs were pushing through thousands of pounds of air that kept him from moving quickly to reach the door and open... it... up... and... pull.... the.... baby.... to... safety...

"Tyler! What? What is it?"

He opened his eyes. Ingrid was shaking his arm and staring at him in the dim light of the candle they had left burning on the bedside table.

"Nothing." He wiped the sweat from his neck and chest with the hem of the bed sheet. "Just a recurring nightmare." The recurring nightmare of his life.

"And what is your nightmare about?"

"I – I can't talk about it." Just the thought of speaking his dreams aloud to someone brought fresh beads of perspiration to his forehead. Never once, since he'd left London, had he told anyone about the events that haunted him. Not even during those early days on Grenada when he rarely slept, before he had discovered that he could make his nightmares recede into the darkest recesses of his mind's attic by consuming vast quantities of rum.

"You should. It helps to get over it if you talk about it." Ingrid was mumbling now, only half awake and drifting back into the sleep he had broken.

How had this happened to him? He had worked so hard to put it behind him, but the truth was, he had only pushed it all away. Now the demons had reared their ugly heads again and this time he was going to have to fight them.

CHAPTER SEVEN

The mid–morning sun created a blinding glare on the surface of the choppy water. Defying the waves and wind without the grace of a sailboat, the small speedboat rose and fell hard against the current as it set a course for the island across the channel.

Tyler looked back at Calvin, who was wearing wrap–around sunglasses and trying to appear nonchalant about the crossing when in fact it was a one–of–a kind outing for an islander who rarely could afford to leave the island. Catching Tyler's eye, he threw his head back and laughed with the sheer delight of the adventure and, despite his own misgivings, Tyler could not help but laugh with him.

He had no idea what they were going to do when they made landfall on Mustique. Christ, he didn't even have a fucking map of the island. The only thing he'd ever heard about on Mustique was a famous place called Basil's Bar and as long as he knew there was a bar he could retreat to, he didn't really care about much else.

A loose game plan was forming in his mind, but it was hard to concentrate as Calvin's friend, Drake, pushed the small outboard motor to its limits, trying to impress them with its minimal power, mostly succeeding in bouncing them against the hard seats and drenching them with sea spray.

As the island grew larger in front of them, Tyler glanced over his shoulder at Bequia in the distance. Mustique was clearly much smaller and, from the look of some of the estates built upon the steep hillsides, much more exclusive. Because both islands were part of the same country, St. Vincent and the Grenadines, they would not need to clear customs or declare the purpose of their visit.

"I drop you off at the bay near town," Drake shouted over the engine, as he began to ease the small craft towards a gleaming crescent of white sand. "That way you can get some transport to where you are going. Or some directions if you are going on foot."

The realization of how clueless he was gave Tyler a sudden headache. He closed his eyes and forced his mind to go blank until the pain subsided. He would have to play this one on instinct. It wouldn't be the first time he had done so, just the first time in a while.

An hour later, fortified by a couple of Hairoun beers, they stood sweating under the hot sun at the bottom of a steep driveway a mile and a half from town. They had been told at a small shop in the village that it led up to Kip Kingsley's "villa," and as they climbed the road out of town they had glimpses of an enormous white estate perched on the rocky ledges overlooking the Caribbean.

Resting in the shade of an almond tree, Tyler discussed his plan of action with Calvin. "I'll go up first without you," he explained. "That way if we need a back–up strategy to get in, you can try and they won't know we're together. And if I don't come back in an hour, you come on up. Either I'll be able to introduce you as my friend or I'll be needing you to get me out of a sticky situation."

"Okay, cool." Calvin nodded his head. "But one thing."

"What's that?"

"I don't have a watch."

A few minutes later, wearing Tyler's wristwatch, Calvin squatted at the base of the tree, looking like any other local worker taking a mid–day rest, and Tyler began the hike up the drive.

After three switchbacks he reached a small parking area where a black jeep sat outside an eight–foot–high, black iron gate set into a concrete wall. Through the bars he could glimpse the sprawling estate inside the enclosure and what appeared to be a large swimming pool.

He stood quietly for a moment, catching his breath and listening for sounds of life. From a cottage across the valley he could hear the bass line of rap music and somewhere down below there was the whine of a saw. The whir of a small plane could be heard faintly in the distance. Birds chirped and the surf roared as it broke against the cliffs, but behind the gate there was only silence.

Tyler followed a narrow path to the right that ran along the outside of the wall before ending abruptly at a sharp drop–off to the sea. Clinging to the end of the wall, he peered around the edge of it for a possible view of anything. He could see a corner of the pool and lounge chairs on a strip of concrete overlooking the Caribbean waters. With sure footing and desperation it might be a potential route in.

He returned to the gate and followed the wall in the opposite direction to the other side of the pool area. On this side there appeared to be a narrow ledge just below the drop–off. Judging by the cigarette butts and bottle caps ground into the dirt, others had stood here before him, spying or eavesdropping on the action inside the compound.

Lowering himself down to the ledge, he found he was at eye level with the cement deck that surrounded the pool. Large sliding doors stood open into the house, beyond which he could see light–colored linen curtains flapping in the breeze, framing the dark mystery of the interior. A bar with a thatched roof was situated off to one side of the pool; a raised wooden platform like a stage was beside it. Tyler found it easy to imagine what kind of debauchery and revelry took place here on occasion.

He sniffed deeply; inside the house someone was cooking a tantalizing curry and the smell reminded him that he hadn't eaten anything yet today.

Back at the gate, he brushed himself off and rang the buzzer on an intercom set into the wall.
Trying to appear nonchalant, but observing carefully, Tyler watched as a huge, muscular black man came out of the front door to the house. His sleeveless white tank top and red nylon shorts displayed his buff physique to its fullest. A shaved head and gold hoops in each ear added to the drama of his don't–fuck–with–me look.

"Yeah, mon," he said from the other side of the iron bars, arms crossed on his chest, with no apparent intention of opening the gate just yet.

"Hey, what's happening. Are Lucy and Kip around?" Tyler wondered if he sounded as ridiculous as he felt.

The big man's nostrils flared as he snorted derisively. "Lucy? No, mon, she not around. "

"Really? She, I mean, they invited me to come by next time I was sailing in the Grenadines. Are they back in the U.K. then?"

"Let me ask you dis, my fren, when de las' time you see Lucy and Kip?"

Tyler had a feeling he had just backed himself into a corner with his casual response. "Actually see them? It's been a few years I guess. Talked to them on the phone more recently than that, emails and what–not, you know. Why? Something up with them?" Tyler put a worried tone into his voice.

"Really? Because if you have been in contact wit' dem you must know den dat Lucy been gone some time now." He was smirking and flexing his muscles.

"That so? Huh. Kip never mentioned it. Always says 'we' and I guess I just assumed..." Tyler tried to change tacks smoothly. "So how about Kip? Can I stop in and say hello to him?"

"Mr. Kingsley not here at de moment."

"Not here meaning not at home or not on Mustique?"

The large man leaned in towards the gate. "If you such good frens wit' him, why don't you just email him and ask for yourself?"

"Well, we don't have email on the boat, that's why," Tyler replied indignantly and then switched tracks again. "Smells like you're cooking up a mean curry in there."

"I'm security, not kitchen help," he replied with a sneering laugh. "And I see enough of you rabid fans to catch on to all your tricks. So tell me your name and I will let Mr. Kingsley know you were here when I see him."

"Ty – Tyburn. Mackie Tyburn." He stuck a hand through the gate. "And you are..."

"Rudy." Rudy's grip left Tyler's fingers nearly paralyzed with a purposeful squeeze. "Nice to meet you, Mackie, now be on your way."

"So tell Kip I'll be around for a few days. Our yacht is anchored out in the harbor. And tell your cook, what's her name...?"

"Lureen?"

"Yes, tell Lureen her curry smells delicious and I can't wait to try some soon. Later, mon." Tyler waved a hand and sauntered off down the steep approach. No, he hadn't gotten inside the walls. But he had information now that might help him do so.

Before long he and Calvin were back in the village at a small snack shop having beef rotis and beers and shooting the breeze with the woman behind the counter who introduced herself as Joselle.

"So you know Lureen who work up at de Kingsley place?" Calvin asked her.

"Sure me know her. She lucky to have dat job wit' her past." Joselle clucked her tongue.

"Really, dat so?" Calvin leaned closer and flashed his beautiful grin. "She got some secrets to hide?"

"You jokin' me, no one have secrets on dis island. Everyone know she have a baby at fourteen with one sailor man who spend a winter here and another at sixteen with one British tourist who spend one week here. She probably have Mr. Kingsley's baby too if him let her." They all laughed with her at that idea although Tyler didn't think it was so improbable.

"She a nice looking lady, dis Lureen?" Calvin asked. "Think she have my baby if I ask her?"

"Not your baby, but maybe his." She nodded towards Tyler. "Seem like she only want babies from white men."

Tyler laughed again and swallowed a mouthful of spicy meat and vegetables. "What about Kingsley? He like the local ladies?"

Joselle nodded vigorously. "We got one here, she become high fashion and move to England wit' him some time ago until he leave her to hook up wit' that little red hair one who have him child but now she gone wit' him again."

"Wait, hold on. Go through that again for me. What's this woman's name?"

"De local one she name Jadene." Joselle was glowing now as she held the rapt attention of two good—looking men. "Mr. Kip Kingsley, he...what they call it...discover her when she just a girl, barely grown into a woman. He take her back to London and she become one famous model, wearing all de dresses with necklines down to here —" Joselle tapped the middle of her own ample belly — " and open on de side up to here." She indicated a spot high on her full hips. "Jadene she nearly six feet tall so she got a lot of long lovely leg to show off. And dat why everyone surprise when he come back wit' de nex' one."

"The next woman? How so?" Tyler was afraid to take another bite of his roti for fear of missing a piece of important information.

"She short, dat one! And not so sexy as Jadene except she like to prance around wit' no top on at de beach and at home too so dey say." Although there was no one else in the shop, Joselle lowered her voice before continuing. "Some say wild t'ings go on up at de Kingsley place. Wild parties – some of de other local girls go some time, you know de kine I mean. Dey all hopin' to get 'discovered' like Jadene but none of them so beautiful enough, even if dey do open dem legs for any man to do."

"So what happened to the little white woman? She still around?" Tyler pressed on towards the information he needed, praying no one else would come into the shop on a hot, still afternoon.

"No, she gone some few years now. Some quarrel between de two and she take de boy and disappear. My sister, Ellen, she used to work up dere, she lose her job at de same time, she was a good fren' of Miss Lucy, even she never hear from her when she gone. And she love dat woman like she her own blood." Joselle shook her head and adjusted the straps of the red tank top that clung to her massive figure.

"That's too bad. What was your sister's job up there?" Tyler slid his empty beer bottle across the counter and she replaced it with another before she went on.

"She clean and cook same as Lureen does now. And she help wit' de boy. But now dat Jadene hanging around again, she glad she not dere. She not like Jadene and all her posing and snobby ways. Jadene she t'ink she too good now to sleep in de two–room house she grow up in. She keep some fancy place in London until Mr. Kingsley take up wit' her again. Some say she famous for posing wit' no clothes on now but what surprise is dat?" Joselle sniffed her disapproval before finishing up with, "And still every one of us on de island want to know what she up to all de time."

"So she is staying up at Kingsley's at this moment?"

"No, dey not expected back until de weekend. Comin' for de Christmas and New Year. But him have a yacht now and so dey spend much of de time out sailing when dey here. Not Jadene so much, she just stay up lounging around de pool and such while him out wit' him friends and him band."

The sound of voices startled the three of them and Joselle had to step out of the spotlight to wait on a group of incoming customers who were then followed by others who needed her attention. Calvin and Tyler thanked her profusely and stepped outside, still absorbing all the information she had provided.

"So what we do now, boss?" Calvin asked. "Talk to that Lureen woman, what I am thinking."

"Yeah, we should find out where she lives and when she gets off work. I bet you could charm that info out of our friend Joselle." Tyler slapped him on the back.

"I am definitely de man for dat job."

Calvin was back moments later but the news was not as sunny as his grin. Lureen lived on the other side of the island and if her schedule was the same as her predecessor, Joselle's sister, she didn't get off work until around five.

"Shit, that means the only way we can talk to her today is to go back up to the house and get past Rudy." Tyler frowned and stared up at the hills. "Which means we need to get Rudy out of there for a few minutes. Now how the hell are we going to do that?"

An hour later Calvin was back on the road to the Kingsley place and Tyler was already hidden behind the almond tree at the bottom of the driveway when a black jeep went speeding past him on its way to town. Apparently Calvin had been convincing in his role as a doctor at the hospital calling to let Rudy know that his elderly mother had been admitted moments earlier for a broken leg and that his signature was needed on some documents before they could treat her.

Tyler sprinted up the driveway and made his way around the property to the ledge overlooking the sea. With a quick foot up on the retaining wall he boosted himself onto the cement deck surrounding the pool. Removing his sandals, he moved stealthily towards the open sliding doors to the house and peered inside.

He was looking at a large open living area furnished with neon pink wicker couches and chairs sporting cushions upholstered in a tropical leaf print of brilliant green. In the center of the room was a large bubbling fish tank in which vibrantly hued fish swam lackadaisically around and around. Lureen was nowhere in sight, however he could hear the sound of a television nearby.

Slipping silently inside, he made his way cautiously across the floor, stopping a few times to take in the artwork on the walls. There were some black and white pornographic photos reminiscent of those he remembered in Kip's London apartment as well as some colorful Caribbean painted versions of similar subjects. A few brought Lucy to mind but he didn't stop to dwell on them.

He stopped at the doorway to the rest of the house, listening carefully before proceeding into what appeared to be an open air dining room with louvered walls held up by bamboo poles. There were two doors out of this room – one led into the kitchen, the other to a long hallway. The kitchen also appeared deserted and well–cleaned; there were no traces of the chicken curry except a faint lingering smell. As he stepped cautiously into the hall, the sounds of the TV grew louder until finally he found the room where Lureen sat on the edge of a bed glued to a local soap opera that was being televised on a contemporary flat screen television.

There was no need to worry about her noticing him moving past the open door; the drama of the show held her undivided attention. He continued on to the end of the hallway to the bedroom that was obviously Kip's. It was up a short staircase, which Tyler though was odd until he realized that it gave the room an unimpeded view above the top of the surrounding walls out onto a deck that overlooked the sea and the other Grenadine islands in the distance. The bed was the largest he'd seen in the Caribbean, at least king–size, but it seemed even bigger, and was made up with silky cotton sheets in aquatic tie–dyed colorations of purples and blues.

But he was not interested in the bed; instead he scanned the dresser and night tables for photographs that might tell tales. Almost immediately one caught his eye – a picture of Lucy nursing a plump baby boy, a beatific look on her face as she gazed down at him.

He couldn't help being astounded at the size of her exposed breasts. He knew that a woman's breasts grew when she was breastfeeding but this was beyond expectation. To confirm that, yes, these did indeed belong to Lucy, there were a few other snapshots of Lucy holding baby Tucker on her hip, naked except for a short sarong, her new enormous breasts taking the focus of the shot, her facial expression soft and rather stoned–looking. He still could not reconcile this Lucy with the type–A–personality journalist he had once known.

But he couldn't linger on those particular photos. Once again, as in London, there was a gallery of shots on the wall, mostly nude black women, mostly obscene poses punctuated by the occasional erotic one. He didn't know what he was learning here, maybe only that Kip's taste in interior decorating hadn't changed in the last five years. It would take some more extensive detective work to find out what he needed to know and there wasn't time for that now.

He put his sandals on and walked loudly back down the hall calling, "Hello? Anybody home?" and stopping at the sight of Lureen's guilty and astounded face.

Lureen's skin had a unique café–au–lait lightness to it, complemented by large golden eyes and a generous mouth. Her straightened hair was streaked blonde and pulled back into a high ponytail that looked like it was tight enough to give her a headache. "Who are you and how did you get in here?" Her voice was childlike and her accent was not nearly as pronounced as many of the others he had spoken to on Mustique.

"Oh, Rudy let me in on his way out. I knocked on the door for a while, but finally just let myself in when no one answered. Good show, I guess," he added, nodding towards the television.

His knowledge of Rudy's name seemed to relax her a little bit. "Well, no one is here until the weekend, you know. Mr. Kingsley not tell me he expecting anyone early. He's coming on Friday and his friends from that Irish band coming Saturday."

That Irish band. Instantly Tyler knew she meant Apoplexica. He could feel his pulse begin to race and he fought the dizziness that came over him whenever their name was mentioned. "Really? I haven't seen any of them in a few years. It will be good to see them all." He hoped she mistook the sweat dripping down the side of his face for a natural reaction to the mid–afternoon heat. "How about Lucy? Will she be here too?"

She stiffened at the mention of Lucy's name. "Lucy be gone more than two years now. You a friend of hers?"

"Well, I used to be. Listen, will you give Kip a message for me? Maybe you should write this down." Tyler had no idea where he was getting the balls to do what he was about to do.

"That's all right. I will remember the message. Go ahead and tell me." Without looking back at the man and woman making love on the television set, she used the remote to lower the sound.

"Tell Kip to bring his boat over to Bequia on Sunday. There's a party happening at De Reef in Lower Bay. Tell his other friends to come too. Will you do that? You can come too if you want."

Lureen blushed and looked down at the tan knee–length skirt she was wearing with a white button–down blouse. "Will you be there?"

Sure and you can have my baby too, Tyler said silently. "Yes, of course," he replied aloud. "What's your name?"

"Lureen. But Mr. Kingsley not usually invite me to be with him and his friends. He prefer the darker girls." She picked at a thread coming loose from her hemline, still not meeting his eye.

"Come with your own friends then. Look, I've got to run. Maybe I'll see you on Sunday. Oh, and invite that other woman who used to work here. What was her name? Ellen?"

She looked up at him then, and a shadow crossed her open face. "Why you want her to come? She not a partying kind of woman."

"Oh, I just remember her from my last visit here, that's all. She was a friend of Lucy's and I liked her." Tyler was speaking rapidly now, trying to keep one ear tuned to any sounds of Rudy's return.

"Well, I won't see her, you know. You might as well ask her yourself. She live on the other side of the island, just past Macaroni Bay in a turquoise house with violet shutters. She and all she children." He could see the thoughts of Ellen moving out of her mind and being replaced by more flirtatious intentions. "So you are from Bequia then?"

"For the moment, you might say. Look, I have to run. You will give Kip the message, yes? Actually, why don't you give me the phone number here and I can call and check up on him before then."

Moments later, after a scrap of paper had been pressed into his hand and held there just long enough to convey Lureen's personal invitation for more of whatever, she opened the front gate for him and Tyler strolled confidently down the driveway. A hot and irritated Calvin met him halfway.

"Everyt'ing cool? Because we haf to go. De boat waiting for us – Marvin haf to be back in Paget Farm by four o'clock." Calvin looked longingly up at Kip's house, obviously wishing he'd had a chance to see inside.

"Guess we will have to come back again then. I wanted to talk to Ellen, who used to work here. Maybe we can get you into the house on our next visit." Tyler started to put his arm around Calvin's shoulder when he suddenly heard the noise of a vehicle gunning its engine up the hill. "Get down. Now." He pulled Calvin over the embankment next to the paved driveway and they flattened themselves face down in the prickly brush as the jeep raced angrily by.

"Him not a happy man," Calvin commented as the dust settled. "You not get back in there again easily."

The two of them stood up and brushed the dirt off their clothes for the umpteenth time that day. "Let's grab another drink before we go," Tyler suggested. And as they walked briskly back into town, he realized that, despite his nervous exhaustion, it felt great to be working again.

CHAPTER EIGHT

Something was tickling his cheek. He swatted and swatted yet still it returned, like a persistent spider web trailing across his face. With an angry gasp Tyler awoke and sat upright in bed groping at the loose mosquito net that was grazing his skin. Apparently he had only gotten as far as untying the neat knot of it above his head before he had passed out on top of the sheets the night before.

The soft sound of snoring startled him again until he realized that Calvin was stretched out fully clothed across the foot of the bed. Falling back onto the damp pillows, he had a vague memory of stumbling back to his room at the Frangipani with Calvin after they had been thrown out of a bar near the harbor at closing time.

His head pounded like a mineshaft in the middle of an excavation; the musty cave–like taste in his mouth seemed to confirm that he must be several miles below the surface of the earth. He had no idea how much they had drunk or what it had been, but whatever it was he had reached a new level of how low he could sink into the black hole of alcohol. Whatever kind of good time he might have had, it couldn't possibly have been worth feeling this bad.

Mornings like this made him actually consider that maybe he ought to stop drinking. Or at least drink less. He wished it was as easy to do it as it was to think about doing it.

Half an hour later, a third cup of coffee in hand, he wandered down to the Internet café to check his email. He had no idea what time it was, Calvin was still wearing his watch, but from the heat of the sun and the number of shops that were open he had to assume it was well beyond ten. The digital readout in the corner of the computer confirmed that it was late enough for him to walk into a restaurant and order lunch instead of breakfast without raising any eyebrows.

As he'd expected, there was another email from Amelia with questions about how he was progressing. His vision, which was always a bit out of focus these days when it came to small print, was worse than usual this morning. The words on the screen seemed to be pulsing with a life of their own; it was hard for him to concentrate. As he scrolled down, his eyes fixated on a single word in the third paragraph, a word that seemed to be haunting him relentlessly every day since he'd arrived on Bequia. Apoplexica.

"I saw an article in the Times yesterday about that Irish band, Apoplexica," Amelia wrote, "and how they had bought a house and sound studio on the island of Bequia. I know that Lucy knew them through Kip; you might check in with them – maybe they know something about where Lucy and Tucker are."

Right, like Lucy would be hanging around with those sleaze bags. Sweat broke out on his brow and his hands began to shake as he realized he had actually allowed himself to have a thought about Apoplexica. He tried to shut the idea out of his brain, but instead he found he was silently arguing with himself – but you haven't seen Lucy in five years, people change.

Abruptly he turned his back on the screen and looked out at the yachts in the harbor. Everything seemed to mock him – flying from a mast was a flag he had assumed was Italian, but now he saw that it was an Irish flag with a shamrock in the center of its green, white and orange stripes. A dollar bus drove by on the road below, its speakers booming with the heavy metal ska sound that Apoplexica had made their reputation on. A battered cardboard box in the corner of the room that held trash bore the logo "Kerry Gold" for the Irish butter it had transported to the island.

There seemed to be no getting away from it – in order to get rid of his demons, it looked like he was going to have to face them head on. He closed his eyes, took a deep breath and then turned to the computer again, picking up the email where he'd left off.

"I'm glad to hear that you have met some of Lucy's friends," he read, hearing Amelia's British accent in his mind. "Any chance they might let you stay with them for a while? Or perhaps they know of a decent hotel or guesthouse that doesn't cost quite as much as the Frangipani. I am still happy to foot the bills, but it would help if we could economize a bit."

Economize? She had no idea how well he could economize these days. He'd barely slept in his hotel room at all since arriving on the island; her money could certainly be put to better use elsewhere. He wondered how Ingrid and Justine would feel about him crashing with them for – for – for however long it was going to take.

Calvin was gone by the time Tyler returned to the Frangipani. It took him less than five minutes to pack up his few belongings and another five to check out. Walking up the main road, he hailed a shiny purple dollar bus and took a seat between an obese woman holding a large battered basket and a skinny schoolgirl in a pale brown uniform.

Unlike most dollar buses, where the passengers usually sat quietly while being assaulted by loud music, on this bus everyone was talking rapidly in local patois and even shouting at each other, sometimes gesturing animatedly in a way characteristic of the Caribbean. Something had happened on the island, something bad, that much he was able to understand. The word "friendship" cropped up so many times that he finally realized they were referring to "Friendship Bay" in the familiar Bequia way. The conversation barely skipped a beat when he shouted "Lower Bay" and the bus stopped to let him out.

Hiking down the steep, canyon–like hill with its breathtaking views of the harbor, he wondered what could possibly be so dramatic on this two–by–eleven–square–mile piece of coral jutting out of the turquoise sea.

When he reached the flat stretch of road that ran along the beach, he could see a group of men that had gathered by the street corner leading up to Fernando's restaurant. As he approached them, Calvin broke away from the crowd.

"Dem found a body." Calvin seemed about to burst with the news. "Floating by de shore at Friendship. De police down dere now so no one can get near, but de ones who find it say it not dead too long. Two, tree days at most." Calvin could barely breathe, he was so excited.

An unpleasant notion began to take root in Tyler's brain. "Man or woman?" he asked.

Calvin looked at him blankly for a second and then sprinted back to the cluster of villagers. Tyler followed more slowly.

"We not know," Calvin answered him, turning away from the others and falling in step with Tyler. "Don't be t'inking what you are t'inking, mon."

"How do you know what I am thinking? What I am wondering is if there's a guesthouse cheaper than the Frangipani in Lower Bay where I can get a room."

"Not to worry, I am sure you can stay with Ingrid and Justine. So let's drop off your bag and get going." Calvin took Tyler's backpack off his shoulder and heaved it easily onto his own.

"Going where?"

"Don't be foo–foo, mon. You know where we are going."

Fortified by a couple of Heinekens, they hiked back up to the main road, went less than a quarter mile beyond the turnoff to Lower Bay and then headed down towards Friendship Bay on the other side of the island. In the clear atmosphere of the sunny afternoon they could see all the way to Mustique across the distant waters.

"What island is that one up close?" Tyler asked, indicating a small rocky island land not far from the Bequia shoreline.

"Petit Nevis. That's where they cut up the whales. Everyone from all around the island go and party when that happen. See that little bay there? It turn red with whale blood."

Tyler had heard that whaling was part of Bequia's history and culture, but was surprised to learn that it was still being practiced. Calvin explained that the islanders, together as a country, were allowed to catch two whales a year, but were generally lucky to catch one. Every citizen was entitled to a share of the meat. A hundred years earlier whale oil had been a major source of trading income and the whaling industry had been the backbone of Bequia's economy.

"Look up there," Calvin said, changing the subject suddenly. "See that big house built into the cliff? That where Apoplexica, the Irish band, be living soon."

Tyler turned to stare at the outsized mansion that appeared to be hanging off the edge of the jagged rock face of the hill. Reachable only by a driveway with half a dozen switchbacks, it was an ominous cement and glass structure with none of the colorful artistry and wood carvings of the other newer houses on the island. Its most distinctive feature was a tower room with windows on all sides and a widow's walk on top surrounded by a gothic iron fence.

As they watched, a small white car came into view and began descending the driveway. A rush of adrenaline prompted Tyler's survival instincts to kick in, forcing him to turn away and continue walking down the hill. "Let's go, Calvin," he called.

"What? Wait, mon, I want to see who in de car. Maybe one of de band or a famous musician fren' of dem."

Calvin could easily assume the hanging–in–the–street nonchalance that was a natural part of island culture; he stared openly at the car as it passed without calling a bit of attention to himself. Tyler kept moving, careful to continue looking in the opposite direction until the vehicle had gone by.

"Oh, it dem, it surely is," Calvin exclaimed excitedly as he caught up with Tyler. "I recognize de guitar player with de orange hair that stand straight up so; him de driver. Guess they already in de place. Why you walk on so and not even give dem one look?"

Tyler cleared his throat nervously. "History, man. History. I'll tell you some time soon. "

"Yes, well, history soon come, mon, because dis road only lead one way, which mean dey must be headed the same place as we." As they came around a curve, they could see several vehicles including a couple of police Land Rovers parked at odd angles to the narrow strip of beach along the bay. A large crowd of people milled around a little farther on, held back from the crime scene by a couple of officers.

Tyler saw the white car and its occupants parked on the opposite side of the beach road, smoking cigarettes and watching the commotion from behind polarized sunglasses. He doubted they would recognize him in his current persona; his bushy sun–bleached hair streaked with gray, his full beard and his ragged, faded clothing provided as much of a disguise as anyone could have devised. Still he hung back and let Calvin do his island thing, that local schmoozing at which he was so adept.

While Calvin made his way to the front of the crowd, Tyler wandered a short distance off, to scope out the territory of Friendship Bay. The crescent of white sand was about the same length as Lower Bay but much narrower and not nearly as picturesque. Parts of it looked barely wide enough for a beach towel and in places the water looked shallow and full of seaweed. A large well–manicured resort occupied one end of the beach, with a restaurant and open–air bar. Another hotel of some sort was at the opposite end and there was a liberal sprinkling of houses on the shoreline between.

Just a few sailboats were anchored farther out in the bay on this windward side of the island. He reasoned that since the customs and immigration offices were in Port Elizabeth all the way around on the leeward side, it was possible that the yachties who anchored here did not come ashore. And with no shore patrol or coast guard, there was no telling who or what might be going on in Friendship Bay.

"Tyler!"

Fuck, Tyler thought. By walking away, he had given Calvin the opportunity to announce his identity to the world. He breathed deeply, assuring himself that there was no reason for alarm.

"De body be a man, a white man. And some say he been shot once in de head."

A man. The dispelling of the unspoken fear that had propelled both of them to the crime scene left Tyler feeling almost giddy with relief. It was not a short, freckled woman with curly blonde or red hair. "Anybody know him?"

Calvin shook his head. "Some t'ink he was shot and dumped off a boat into de sea. But he surely didn't die from drowning."

"Do they know how long ago?" Tyler could not imagine how ancient the forensic science techniques might be on an island this size with virtually no crime.

"Not very long; de body still in good shape. Maybe one, two days. Dey waiting on some guys from St. Vincent to come do dat kine work." Calvin's face broke into a sudden grin. "Oh, and you know what else? De whole of Apoplexica comin' down for de Christmas holiday to stay. And dey be playin' at de Reef for Old Year's Night. Yes, mon, we got our own celebrities on dis islan' just like Mustique now. Just like Mustique."

With the helpless feeling of being sucked into the vortex of a storm, Tyler realized there was no turning back now. He could either leave the island immediately or face the music. Literally.

"It look as if Ingrid is still at de school," Calvin remarked as they passed through the cluster of buildings that loosely comprised the village of Lower Bay. "Maybe we should stop and axe her if you can stay wit' her. Jus' to make it right, you know."

The shutters on the windows of the Sunny Island Primary School were indeed still propped open and Tyler and Calvin stopped to peer inside. On the far side of the room, Ingrid was typing rapidly on a computer keyboard.

"Hey, sexy lady!" Calvin called.

Startled, Ingrid looked over her shoulder. "Oh, hi, come on in." As they approached, she quickly shut down whatever program she had been working on and it crossed Tyler's mind that her grin had more than a touch of guilt in it. "What brings you boys back to school? Need a few lessons in something?" Standing, she gave Tyler a warm kiss on the mouth.

"Oh, I could probably use a refresher on a few things." He laughed as he looked over her shoulder, straining his eyes for any clues as to what she had been working on. An icon in the corner of the screen indicated that the computer was connected to the Internet. "Can you get online here?"

"Yes, of course. We may be small, but we are up–to–date. How was Mustique?"

"Interesting. Tell you about it later."

"Does that mean you're coming by for a visit?" she teased.

"Actually, him need more den a visit. Him need to use de spare bed for a bit."

Tyler was glad that Calvin had jumped right to the issue at hand. "Is that a problem? It would save Lucy's sister a bunch of money."

Ingrid paused for a fraction of a second before responding. "It's only a problem if you sleep in the guest bed instead of mine." She squeezed his buttocks suggestively. "Now go on up there and get naked. I'll be home in ten minutes."

As they started up the hill to the house, Tyler tapped Calvin on the shoulder and put a finger to his lips. Quietly he moved back to the school and looked intently through the nearest window. Ingrid was back at the computer, typing fast and furiously into what appeared to be an email. Slipping away from the building, he rejoined Calvin who waited patiently in the middle of the road.

"So. You are one of them man who lose themselves into the love of the drinking, Mr. Mackenzie."

From his prone position on the wicker couch, Tyler turned his head towards the sound of Justine's voice. She was not looking at him; instead she was studying the half–finished watercolor painting on the easel in front of her. He thought perhaps he had imagined she was speaking to him and so he did not reply.

"How long you been this way? I know you not been like so your whole lifetime."

She was addressing him, but the way she was talking she might as well have been speaking to herself. Her voice was soft and intimate, inviting him to respond. Without making a sound, she gently placed a couple of brush strokes on the canvas and then stood back from it again.

His hand was wet from the condensation on the outside of the glass he was holding, as the heat of his body and the warmth of the rum melted the ice cubes inside. Without lifting it to his lips, he could taste its sweetness on his tongue, its comforting sensation was his closest friend and confidant. He did not have to answer her; he could just take another mouthful and relax in the enveloping intensity of its embrace.

"Was it a woman? A woman who reject you? A lot of times it is a woman make a man drown himself like you doing." Justine was still talking to her painting. The light in the room was fading; Tyler realized the sun had already set.

Justine switched on the lamp that hung above her head and suddenly she and her work were illuminated in a dazzling spotlight that left Tyler sitting in the shadows outside her circle of brightness. She was wearing the brilliant green skirt again and as she swayed back and forth examining her creative output, she reminded him of a mermaid, a seductive siren calling him to crash his boat on the rocky shoals of her shores.

"No," he heard himself saying. "No, it wasn't a woman."

Justine made a clucking sound in the back of her throat and then dabbed a swath of robin's egg blue across the background. "Not a woman? Then what then?"

What then... Did he dare to say it aloud? Not since the day it had happened had he ever spoken of the event that had driven him into a bottle of rum on another continent in another hemisphere.

"Wait, let me guess...if it was not a woman, then maybe you lost your job? Or a family member? Or maybe you failed at something big you were trying to accomplish." As she spoke, she outlined the robin's egg blue with a band of royal purple.

"A failure, yes. That's what it was. A big fat failure." Although he had never thought about it that way, it was a perfect description of what had happened.

"Well, you know what they say about failure. You can't know success without it."

"Oh, I had plenty of successes before this failure." He laughed harshly and took a deep swallow of rum.

"Did you now? So what did a successful man like yourself fail so miserably at then?"

Tears began to run silently down his cheeks, following the path with which, five years before, they had become so familiar. "I couldn't save them," he whispered. "They died because of me and I couldn't save them."

Justine finally turned to look at him, her brown eyes becoming wells of concern in her smooth, placid face. "Who died?" she asked, putting down her paintbrush and kneeling on the floor next to the couch.

"I don't even know their names. One minute they were there and the next minute – boom, they were gone." As the memories overwhelmed him with their intensity, his brain started to grow black inside as it tried to shut down. His drink slipped from his fingers and fell over onto his chest, drenching his T–shirt with its icy wetness. "Shit."

As Justine picked up the glass, Tyler sat up, angrily whipping the shirt over his head and using it to dry the hot tears on his face. "Sorry, obviously I can't really talk about it. I never have."

"And I would say obviously you can talk about it, because you just did." Justine sat down on the part of the couch where his head had been, so that he could not recline again. He could feel the reassuring softness of her arm and shoulder against his back. Pulling his knees up, he leaned his elbows against them and curled into himself.

He had exposed his deepest, rawest wound to her and she would not let it be. "Tell me," she said. "Where did this happen? This 'boom and they were gone'."

For half a minute or so her question hung over them like a heavy rain cloud. He wanted her just to go away and leave him alone, but he knew she wouldn't, she was going to keep at him, just like this island kept battering him with references and incidents from his past. At last, without raising his head, he mumbled a reply.

"London."

"Okay, then. And how long ago it was?"

"Five years and counting."

"So five years in the past some people died who you didn't know and couldn't help. Doesn't that happen every day somewhere in the world?"

He studied his toes; long, dirty and covered with tough brown skin and a sprinkling of golden hairs. One of the nails was an ugly blackish–purple where he had run into a piece of coral on the beach at night. "No, this was different," he answered at last. "I was the one who was supposed to die. They died by ... mistake." The last word stuck in his throat and then came out as whisper.

"Mistake," Justine repeated flatly and unemotionally. "You mean, someone was trying to kill you?"

He nodded and swallowed hard.

"But why?"

"Because I had found out something about them they didn't want anybody to know." All the memories of that time came rushing back clearly now; the speed and sharpness with which he had lived his life as a journalist pierced him like the pointed pencils he had used back then to jot down notes on stories.

As though she were the reporter, Justine asked him one more question, the all–important one. "Who?"

And with a whooshing feeling of letting go, as though he were skydiving, he quietly said the name. "Apoplexica."

CHAPTER NINE

Twenty–four hours later, the four of them sat around the kitchen table, eating curried conch and discussing what they thought Tyler should do next. The others were a colorful group – Ingrid, still in her turquoise bikini top and sarong, refreshed by a sunset swim, Justine with a streak of blue paint across one cheek, Calvin wearing a yellow nylon cap that advertised Banks Beer from Barbados.

Tyler, in contrast, was a study in subtle earth tones – khaki shorts, tawny eyes, bleached–out hair and beard – yet inside he felt brighter than he had in years. On top of it all, he was ravenous. And his hunger had as much to do with his new state of mind as it did with the fact that he hadn't eaten anything since the previous day.

They had talked nearly till dawn, he and Justine. Once he'd gotten started, he could not stop and the story poured out of him like bath water going down a drain. He told her everything, starting with how Lucy had seduced him into taking on the lead she'd been asked to investigate about a terrorist faction in London that was rumored to be funded, and possibly run by, someone in the rock music business. It was too close to home, she had said, she was afraid of making enemies in her new world, afraid of the mess she knew the English tabloids could make of her own life and of Kip's career. But she had learned enough to know that it was a story that needed to be told and she thought Tyler should take it on.

It only took a few weeks before the threats started appearing in his mailbox and on his message machine. By the time he had narrowed the possible suspects down to two bands, the warnings had become more intimidating. The day after he followed Ethan Sands to a seedy pub not far from Gatwick Airport and observed his meeting with a couple of neo–Nazi types, Tyler was pushed off a street corner in front of a bus and only just missed being run over.

He had worked on dangerous assignments before and had always managed to squeeze out of harm's way, sometimes just barely, before turning in his story. But he had never dealt with terrorists before. As it became clearer and clearer that Apoplexica was heavily involved, he began to realize that he was onto something much bigger than he'd imagined.

And then one morning he'd walked out of his flat and headed for his car which was parked across the road. After he'd opened the driver's door, he realized he'd forgotten his laptop and had slammed the door shut again. His peripheral vision registered a young mother pushing her baby in a pram along the sidewalk as he sprinted back up to the flat and inserted his key in the lock.

The explosion that shook the stairwell was deafening. At the same time, the glass door to the building shattered as a piece of twisted metal from the car hood launched through it after hurling twenty feet across the narrow street. Leaping through the jagged shards of the doorframe, Tyler had stopped short, unable to absorb the horror of the bloody remains of the mother and baby on the sidewalk next to the burning wreckage of what had been his car. They were now the accidental victims of a bomb that had obviously been intended for him, a timed device that he had activated upon opening the driver's door.

He remembered two of his neighbors restraining him, taking him inside to wait in someone else's living room for the police to come. Despite the numbing shock he was in, he had enough wits about him to know that the game was over. It was bad enough that Apoplexica wanted him silenced and would go to any lengths to make it happen. But when innocent people died because of Tyler's actions, things had gone too far. If he implicated the band now, he was writing his own death sentence and it apparently didn't matter how many bystanders got in the way.

When the police arrived he told them that it must have been a random street bombing; he had no idea why his car had been chosen. He was not about to involve the publication for whom he had been freelancing the story. When they were finally done questioning him, he was in such an agitated state internally that he staggered back to his own rooms, unsure of what to do next or even what he could safely touch.

Everything looked to him like a possible trigger for a bomb. His refrigerator door, the TV remote, the laptop that had saved his life at the cost of two others. The blinking light on his telephone letting him know there was another message waiting, probably from his would–be killers. He wasn't safe here, nor was anybody he came in contact with.

Collapsing on the couch, he closed his eyes. Instantly he was assaulted by an image of a tiny baby's bleeding hand beneath the fractured structure of a flaming pram. Breaking into a sweat, he was on his feet in a flash, pacing the small room. He had to get out of there, had to get away from his life, had to escape from himself. But first he had to erase everything on his computer that had to do with the terrorism story and with Apoplexica.

In the end, he took a hammer to the laptop, dumping the pieces in a rubbish bin in Victoria Station on his way to Heathrow. By midnight he was on a plane to Barbados. By morning he was standing on the beach in Grenada, drinking a shot of rum.

Justine had not said much but she listened attentively, occasionally asking him a probing question to keep him talking and remembering. Once during the recounting of his tale, Tyler began to shiver and discovered that his bare chest was suddenly glowing with the sheen of cold sweat. A light blanket materialized in Justine's hands, which she gently wrapped around his shoulders before urging him to continue. When Ingrid peered around the corner questioningly, she signaled with a slight but significant tilting of her head that Ingrid should leave them alone.

By the time Tyler finished his narrative, his legs and arms were jerking and twitching in a random nervous pattern. Kneeling on the floor in front of him, Justine took both his hands in her own and held them tightly in a safe and soothing way, at the same time forcing him to meet her gaze. When she spoke, the melody of her smooth voice contrasted with the insight of her knife–like words.

"So Apoplexica is here on this island. And strangely enough, here you are too. Do you think they still want to see you dead?"

For a moment he felt as weak as a six–year–old cornered by bullies on the playground. He nodded as his eyes began to fill with tears again.

"So what are you going to do about it?"

He'd let Apoplexica destroy his former life; his own self–destructive behavior was destroying his present existence. What did he have left to lose? And then suddenly he remembered.

"Fight back," he whispered. He sat up straighter and cleared his throat. "Bust the fucking bastards. Find Lucy and Tucker."

She squeezed his fingers reassuringly. "All right. Yes, mon. That's what we want to hear. Now what will you do to make that happen?"

"I don't have a fucking clue," he admitted, the ghost of a grin starting to turn up the corners of his mouth. "Will you help me?"

A laugh erupted from deep within Justine. The sound of it filled Tyler with an unexpected warmth. "I am no detective journalist woman, you know. But, of course I will help you. We all will."

Just before dawn, he'd fallen asleep on the couch. When he awoke it was mid–afternoon and he realized that his sleep had been deep and dreamless for the first time in days, possibly in years.

"So, Mr. Investigator." Calvin washed down the last bit of spicy conch with a mouthful of Hairoun beer. "What is de plan?"

"Well, I've been thinking." Tyler did not want to admit how long it had been since he had actually spent any time thinking. But today he had sat on the deck and even organized his thoughts on paper before everyone had arrived home a few hours before. "The most important thing here is that we find Lucy and Tucker and make sure they are safe."

The half–second pause before Ingrid responded was not lost on Tyler. "Okay. How do you propose we do that?"

His eyes met hers but her steady gaze revealed nothing. "In my opinion, the first step is to make sure she is not back with Kip. Then, given the timing of her disappearance with the arrival of Apoplexica on this island, we figure how to check out that angle."

"Why do you think she never told us about Tucker being Kingsley's boy?" Justine asked without looking up as she sketched an abstract design on a paper napkin.

"It's a small island. Maybe she didn't want the word to get around." Tyler was discretely watching all three of them for signs of falsehoods.

"Him treat her badly, mon. You know she afraid for she and de boy when she get here," Calvin exclaimed, looking from Ingrid to Justine.

"How did she get here? Does anybody know?"

Ingrid shook her head. "We never asked. She didn't like to talk about her past. Once she told me she had left an abusive relationship and didn't want to look back."

"Do you think he beat her?"

"She have marks on her when she first come." Calvin's face seemed to turn a shade darker.

Tyler suddenly felt a bit queasy. "Marks?"

"Around her wrists and ankles, bruised—up like. Black and blue."

Justine looked up, genuine surprise on her face. "I never knew that. Sounds like some sort of bondage thing."

Ingrid shuddered. "Do you think? That's a bit extreme."

"Anywhere else?"

Calvin nodded grimly. "Around she titties." He drew two wide circles on his own chest demonstrating what he meant.

"How'd you see those?" Justine teased him, half joking, half truly curious.

"You know she not a modest one, dat Ruby. First time I met her on Lower Bay Beach, she topless. Before she realize it not really what de women do here." Calvin sucked on his beer bottle, seeing Lucy in the distance of his memory. "Remember she have dem giant ones too, when she first come here. It hard not to look at dem."

Recalling the photograph in the Fed Ex envelope, Tyler knew what he meant. "What about Tucker? Any marks on him?"

"Not that I ever saw," Ingrid commented. "Calvin?"

"No. De boy seem pretty okay. Never leave him mama side for a long time it seem. Dey always keep an eye on each other."

"Still. She was married to Kip, right?" Justine stopped drawing and looked up. "Women go back to abusive relationships all the time."

"But we know from our trip to Mustique that they haven't gotten back together. Everyone told us so." A new thought crossed Tyler's mind. "Do you think he saw her when he was here playing on Bequia? Maybe he had Apoplexica pick her up."

"What he need her for now?" Calvin scoffed. "Him with dat black Mustique woman dem told us about."

"Yes, but he could still want to punish Ruby for leaving him," Justine explained. She seemed to have a deeper understanding of this sort of situation than might be expected. She looked at Tyler. "And from what you've told me, who could do that better than Apoplexica?"

Her suggestion made Tyler feel suddenly raw—edged and ragged. Reaching for another Hairoun, he said, "We've got to get into that house in Friendship Bay."

"You're a little bit in love with her, aren't you?"

"What?"

Tyler opened his eyes to stare at Ingrid on the pillow beside him, silhouetted in the moonlight. She was propped up on one elbow, her cheek resting in one hand, her breasts falling softly to one side, while she gently ran her fingers through the coarse curls on the back of his head.

"Who?" he asked this time, licking his lips where the taste of their recent sexual activity still lingered.

"Justine. I saw how you looked at her." Ingrid's fingers stopped their stroking as he sat up and pulled away from her.

"Justine?" It was true, he did feel a newfound closeness with her after the previous night and it was a very different sort of intimacy than he had with Ingrid. But in love?

"It's okay. I am too." With gentle forcefulness, Ingrid pushed him back down into a reclining position again. "She's pretty special. But so far, I've never known her to let anyone in. Man or woman."

Tyler did not reply for a minute, as he absorbed all the information Ingrid had just hinted at. He recalled that during their first conversation, Ingrid had said something about being in love with someone that she couldn't have. Had she been talking about Justine?

"So? Does that turn you off or turn you on?"

He chuckled a little at her bold assumptions. "What? The idea that you might be in love with a woman?"

"One that you might be in love with too?"

A erotic image of a menage–a–trois flashed briefly through his mind. "No, that's just confusing," he replied, pushing the concept aside. "Are you telling me then that you live with a woman who you would like to be lovers with but she won't have you? Doesn't that drive you crazy?"

"I deal with it. What do you think you're doing in my bed?"

"Ouch! That's a bit harsh!" But not surprising, he thought.

"What did you say, a bit hard?" she teased, reaching for him beneath the sheets. "Seems like the idea excites you a little, yes?" True enough, their discussion had aroused him again.

But this time as she threw her leg over him, their simple sexual attraction was infinitely more complicated than it had been ten minutes before.

"You are one crazy man!" Justine exclaimed when he told her his plan the next morning. "Why do you think that will work?"

"Because their egos are so big. Even if they hadn't thought of the idea before, it will appeal to at least one of them. And as a matter of fact, so will you." Tyler rinsed the last of the breakfast dishes and dried his hands on a striped towel.

"What?"

"Appeal to at least one of them. Wear that top you have on right now and you'll be inside that house in no time." Tyler grinned and waited to see how Justine would react to his comment about the snug–fitting, black tank top she was wearing with the loose pair of boxers she had apparently slept in.

Blushing, she let out an angry stream of patois she knew he would not understand. Finally stopping for a breath, she tilted her head to contemplate him, the dozens of tiny braids still dancing from her tirade. "So you think they will let a local woman artist in to paint a mural of themselves on a wall of their big fancy mansion just because she is sexy?"

"Not only because she is sexy, but also because she is smart and talented and acts like she knows what she is doing." As Tyler knew from experience, the latter was truly the key to pulling the job off. "Now what we need to do is find you a picture of their logo, which I recall looks something like a big ball of fire. Do you have any of their CDs around?"

"Not me. I don't like their sound. But Ingrid might." Justine led the way into the living room to where their combined collection of music was kept. "See what you can find. I am going to get dressed."

"Put on something a heavy metal grunge band might like a woman to wear!" he called after her.

"I don't have any dog collars or chains," she called back, shutting the door to her room.

Tyler walked with her to the top of the hill, carrying her bag of art supplies. In the clear, unhurried reality of life on an island baking slowly in the mid–day sun, their plan seemed naïve and implausible. Justine would literally knock on the door of Apoplexica's mansion and claim she was there because someone had ordered a wall mural and she needed to see where they wanted it painted. If none of the band was home, hopefully she could persuade one of the hired help (assuming they had

111

a maid or a cook) to let her scope out a possible site. The least it might do was give them an inkling if Lucy and Tucker were there or had ever been there. The most it might do...well, the possibilities were endless.

He didn't dare go any farther with her than the end of the Lower Bay road. Handing over the paint–splattered tote, he smiled encouragingly and said, "You look fabulous."

She was dressed in an exotic–looking outfit consisting of long silky swaths of blue and green fabrics that draped and flowed in loose points around her arms and legs. A matching turban and lots of dangling shiny jewelry added to the dazzling effect. Like a powerful sorceress, he thought, watching her move up the hill towards the turnoff for Friendship Bay. Let's hope she can enchant Apoplexica the same way she does the rest of the world.

Damn, he wished he could go with her. Now all he could do was wait.

There was only one way to sit still when he was this nervous. He tried to drink his beer slowly, but every time he finished one, Moses would put another one in front of him. At least if he stuck with beer, his mind wouldn't get quite so fuzzy. He couldn't remember if he'd had four or five by the time he decided a nap on the beach was in order.

He had no idea how long he'd slept in the shade of the manchioneal trees when a tickling sensation up and down his back awoke him. Instinctlvely, he flung an arm out to swat whatever was crawling on him and instead came in full contact with the soft warm flesh of a woman's belly. Forcing his eyes open, he saw Ingrid kneeling on the sand next to him, laughing mischievously.

"Resting up for tonight, lover boy?"

He guessed it must already be late afternoon; she was wearing her bikini and there were no children in sight. He rolled over and licked his dry lips with a tongue that felt swollen from dehydration. For the first time in a long while, he realized how much he hated feeling like this before the sun even went down.

"You been home?" he asked hoarsely, propping himself up on his elbows and looking around the beach.

"Just to change my clothes. Why?"

"I was wondering if Justine was back yet."

"Back from where?"

His roving gaze came to rest on the bottle of water in her net beach bag. Reaching across her sandy thighs, he helped himself to several mouthfuls before replying.

"Friendship Bay. She went to the band's house."

"She what?"

He could not decipher the expression on Ingrid's face as he explained the plan of which Justine was such an integral part. Jealousy, fury, worry, disgust...he thought he saw all of these emotions cross her face and then disappear into her hard, Nordic cheekbones.

"You seem to have a problem with this scheme, my dear," he remarked, stroking the curve of her bare torso with his forefinger.

"I can't believe you would put Justine in danger like that." Abruptly, she pulled away from his touch and stood up.

"It's not dangerous. What are you doing?"

Ingrid was packing up her possessions and brushing the sand off her legs with the edge of her sarong. "I'm going over there to find her," she said. "Make sure she's all right."

"You can't do that." Tyler leaped to his feet, trying to ignore the flash of dizziness he experienced from the quick change to his fragile equilibrium. "We don't want them to know you two are connected. You're going to have your own part to play in all this." He had no clear picture yet what Ingrid's role would be, but her day was definitely coming.

"Really." She froze for a few seconds, her feelings still hidden behind a steely mask. "And when do I come into your plan?"

"No later than Sunday," he said, making it up as he went along. "You've got to get them to De Reef if they weren't already planning it and then you've got to pick one of them to get really close to. The same way you got really close to me."

He wasn't sure how she was going to react to what he was subtly suggesting, but he had a feeling that sleeping with a rock star was definitely on her lifetime list of things she wanted to do. And it appealed to her competitive nature – especially now that she knew that Lucy had lived with Kip, and Justine was already (hopefully) inside those foreboding concrete walls.

Ingrid's face softened as she contemplated his words. "You think I could do that? Be like...who was that famous woman spy?"

"Mata Hari? I'm counting on it."

"Okay, then." She let her bag fall back into the sand. "But if Justine is not back by dark, you better figure out a reason why I am going over there tonight." She left no question as to who, in the greater scheme of things, she cared about the most. Although he still knew so little about Ingrid, he definitely knew that.

"Absolutely. But I'm sure she's fine," he promised, trying to convince himself as much as her. "Now how about I buy you a beer?"

CHAPTER TEN

By nightfall, Tyler and Ingrid had made their way home only to discover that Justine was not back yet. Tyler was as worried as Ingrid, but put his energy into distracting them both by stripping off her swimsuit and dancing her backwards into the bedroom. Ingrid could not hold her liquor as well as Tyler and he used this to his advantage. And the fact that he knew her sexually better than any other way. As she alternately sighed and shrieked with pleasure beneath him, he heard the outside screen door slam. Justine had returned. Ingrid heard nothing through the frenzy of her orgasm and afterwards fell instantly into a contented dreamless slumber.

Brushing away the damp hairs sticking to her wet brow, he gently covered her with a sheet so that she would not be cold when the rivulets of sweat coursing between her breasts dried; then he tiptoed out of the room.

Justine was in the kitchen, unwinding her colorful turban, sipping some tonic water with lime. "Where your clothes, boy?" she asked, giving his naked body a once over before turning away.

Tyler reddened and returned to the bedroom for his shorts. Clearly, he was starting to feel very at home here.

"So tell me, tell me, tell me!" he whispered loudly. "How did it go? And what have you been doing there all this time?"

"Oh, nothing. Only becoming best friends with Mrs. Ethan Sands." She winked at him and undid the straps on her sandals.

"MRS. Ethan Sands? He has a wife? Tell all!"
Eagerly, Tyler straddled the chair next to her.

"Hmmm....All? All is worth a lot, my friend." She
rubbed at one of the indentations the sandal strap had
left across her foot. "Plus the cab fare from Friendship
to here. And it cost an extra ten EC after dark."

"Okay. Okay. Just start at the beginning."

"Just so you know, it did not start off well." Justine
told him about being let into a cavernous hallway by an
elderly woman from the village called La Pompe and
whom she knew as a friend of her family. At first she
was afraid that this woman, called Cecily, would reveal
something about Justine that she shouldn't, but then
she realized there was nothing to hide. She was playing
herself, an artist on a mission, and there was no reason
for Cecily to know more than that.

Cecily immediately assumed it was "him wife" that
was adding a hand–painted mural to the interior design
and soon Justine was having a cool drink in a steel and
glass kitchen with Eileen Sands, who apologized for
entertaining her in such a casual way, but so far it was
the only room with real chairs. The living and dining
room furniture had been special–ordered from a
Thailand imports company and had yet to arrive.

"What does she look like?"

"Eileen? She is so very thin, bony like a skeleton,
and she have this long face and short, short black–as–
midnight hair that stand up straight from her head in
places like so and – wait a minute." Justine reached for
the sketchbook peeking from her tote and flipped
quickly through it. "This is her." She passed it across
the table to him.

Tyler found himself looking at a pencil drawing that
skillfully blended waif–like youthfulness with the
haggard lines of hard partying. Dark eyes, a petite
nose, and a narrow mouth. She appeared to be wearing
a black vest held together with laces and a short skirt
that displayed lanky, twig–like legs.

"It all leather," Justine commented and Tyler could not interpret whether her tone was admiration or disdain.

"You're very good. Did she see this?"

"Yes, of course, mon. How else she going to hire me if she doesn't see what I can do?"

Apparently Justine had played her cards so smoothly that Eileen Sands didn't care how she happened to show up or why. Over the course of the afternoon, and a couple of large spliffs shared with Tara, the girlfriend of one of the other band members, Eileen proceeded to engage Justine's services as a color consultant, muralist and portrait artist.

"Yes sir, Mr. Mackenzie. This little plan of yours will be paying my rent for the next six months." Behind her expression of practiced sophistication, Justine's eyes glowed with delight.

Tyler laughed. "Remind me again, who owes who for this?"

"I am exhausted, mon! Had to spend all of my day and night chatting up these two foolish women! I am not like her–" she nodded towards Ingrid's room, "– just because they are with famous men does not make their friendship valuable to me."

"Speaking of the famous men," Tyler's tone became serious again, "were they there?"

"They just like all the male species. When dinner time come, they show up to fill their bellies. Yes, I met them."

"And what were they like?"

"Too old for the way they act. Potbellied middle–age men with dyed hair behaving like they college boys. They don't impress me much." Justine sniffed her disapproval. "Hard to believe they smart enough to come up with whatever contraband scheme you think they do."

Tyler laughed a little. "So maybe if they are that stupid, you can get them to say some things they shouldn't."

"Yeah, maybe if I let them show me they manhood. But you will need your friend Ingrid for that job."

"I hope that for now you pretended you were just a little bit interested..."

"Not to worry, mon!" Justine assured him, standing up and stretching. "I am smart enough to know how to hold them close —"she reached a hand out to grab Tyler's arm and pulled herself towards him —"but not too close— " and then stood back at arm's length, still holding on.

"Yes, I bet you are pretty good at that." Her physical proximity was making him wish more than ever that he had met her before he'd slept indiscriminately with her roommate. Grasping the warm hand that touched him, he forced her to meet his gaze, to see what was in his eyes, before letting her move away. He was pleased to see she appeared slightly uncomfortable as she hastened to maintain her safe distance and continue talking.

"So I am going back tomorrow to do some preliminary sketches. And Saturday —"

"And Saturday what?"

"They are all headed over to Mustique to spend the night partying. They invited me to come, but I suggested I stay and do some painting while they were away."

"Wait —" Tyler shook his head in disbelief. "They invited you go over to Mustique with them? To Kingsley's? And you said no?"

"I thought it would be a good opportunity for you to come to their house and do some poking around. In–VES–ti–gat–ing. Besides, I am not a big party girl."

"Damn. I know you're not." Tyler frowned and picked at the rough wooden edge of the table. "I just wish there was some way to take advantage of an invitation like that. You have no idea how hard it is to get into that place."

They sat in silence for a half a minute or so before Justine said, "Maybe Ingrid should come by in the afternoon tomorrow. Meet them. Get to know them. Help them sail their yacht across the channel. Eileen could use another girlfriend."

Tyler realized he was suddenly grinning widely and wordlessly as they both sat and thought about what Justine was suggesting. "It's brilliant," he said finally. "Think she'll go for it?"

"Our Ingrid?"

"Should we wake her up now or wait until morning to ask her?"

Without waiting for an answer, Tyler headed into the bedroom.

The next afternoon, moments after school was out, Ingrid was home and preparing to meet Justine at the house in Friendship Bay. The word "excited" barely described how she was conducting herself. Her behavior reminded Tyler of how Lucy had acted when she had first received the assignment to cover Kip's concert tour.

After her initial grumpiness at having been woken from a sound sleep the night before, Ingrid had been thrilled at the idea of getting to know the Apoplexica family and even more elated at the prospect of pulling an all–nighter at one of Kingsley's parties on Mustique.

"You can't be just partying," Tyler had cautioned her. "You have to be on your toes, noticing things, asking questions that don't give anything away, paying attention to more than just what's going on. You have to pay attention to your surroundings as well. I mean, you have to look like you're partying, but you can't get too wasted."

Justine had laughed merrily at the expression on Ingrid's face. "Don't count your chickens," she warned.

"First you must make Eileen or the other one, Tara, like you so much that they can't leave you behind."

"Just watch me tomorrow," Ingrid had promised. "I know how to make friends when I need to."

Now Tyler ripped a sheet of paper out of a small notebook and handed it to her. "Here are some things to keep an eye out for when you're hanging around with the wives and their band of husbands. And here –" he ripped another page out – "are things to ask and look for if you make it as far as Mustique."

Ingrid scanned the lists as she brushed her hair. "So I'm not supposed to have known Lucy, right? I mean, I never knew her as Lucy anyway, it shouldn't be hard."

"Well, there are pictures of her at Kip's. I mean, if you are a fan, you can certainly recognize photos of her as his former girlfriend. But no, don't mention that you found out the woman you knew as Ruby on Bequia was actually Lucy." Was she going to be able to pull this off? No, it would be fine. Ingrid was smart and she could be very deceptive, as Tyler himself knew. Which reminded him of something.

"Would you mind if I used the computer at the school to check my email this afternoon? It would save me from having to walk into town."

Ingrid scowled a little. "The school is all locked up. I supposed I could let you in on my way out and then if you leave by the back door, it will just lock behind you."

"Thanks a lot. That would be great." He stretched out on the bed and watched her pack a few things into a straw shoulder tote; a bathing suit, a pair of purple underpants, a tee shirt and a small sweater. "Hey, how long you planning to be gone for tonight?"

She blushed a little. "You never know. If I can't make it home, I might as well be prepared. In fact –" she added some sunscreen, a toothbrush and a sarong to the bag and then threw in another pair of underpants – "just in case I don't get back until Sunday."

"Until Sunday?" But she was right. It was entirely possible. Damn, he wished he could go with her. Not necessarily for her company, but for the investigating adventure. And to do the job right. "Hey, if Calvin and I show up there at some point, let us in, okay?"

"What? What are you talking about? That isn't part of the plan." Her panicked look reminded him that she was not a professional at this game.

But a new scheme was hatching in his mind. "Here's the thing — if they are all planning to come back here on Sunday to De Reef, then if Calvin and I can get there —"

"You sneaked in before, why can't you do that again? Don't make it too complicated for me." She sat down next to him on the bed and rubbed his bare thigh. "Or will you miss me so much that you can't live without me?"

"No, you're right. You'll do much better there on your own. A single sexy woman can learn a lot more than a sexy woman with a boyfriend." He rested his hand on her waist. "Now what do you think? Do we have time for a quick one before you go?"

To his surprise, she shook her head and stood up. "I can't; it will just sidetrack me. Come on." She held out a suntanned hand to him. "The anticipation will make you that much hotter for me when you see me again. Now let me take you down to the school so I can get on my way."

The darkened schoolroom was unexpectedly cool in the heat of the late afternoon. Situated on the first floor of a two—story house built into a small slope, two sides of the room were cement supporting walls of the foundation. A third was lined with wood—shuttered windows that were flung wide open in the daytime for maximum light; a large double door occupied the fourth wall.

Luckily there were no passwords or security protections on the computer, but it took about five minutes for the dial–up service to fully connect to the internet. While he waited, he explored the computer's files. He remembered the guilty look Ingrid had worn when he startled her a few days earlier. He wondered what websites she had visited lately; hopefully the browser's history would tell him.

He was surprised to find that Ingrid kept the computer extremely well organized. He clicked on a folder called "Progress Reports" and felt strangely disoriented for a minute to see one labeled, "Mackenzie, T." Opening it, he realized immediately that it referred to Lucy's son whom they called Tee and who was known on Bequia by the last name of Mackenzie. It suddenly occurred to him that Lucy had probably used this computer as well. He did a quick search command for anything with the name "Ruby." It led him to a deleted folder that still resided in the Recycle Bin.

It was funny how people always thought their files were gone just because they had dumped them in the trash. Most people rarely emptied the trash in their computer.

As he had suspected, "Ruby's Folder" was still full of files. Tyler scanned the titles, hoping for something that would say "Personal" or "Journal" or, even more improbably, "Itinerary for Leaving Bequia." Most of the documents were lesson plans or worksheets for young children.

The only file he found interesting was the oldest one in the folder. Judging from its date, it appeared to have been created shortly after Lucy had arrived on Bequia. "Dear Ellen," it read. "I just wanted to let you know that we arrived safely and we are fine. Some nice people have taken us in and we are settling into our new life. Thank you for helping; I will never forget what you did for us. I hope someday we will meet again in a better place. Love to you and the kids, L & T." And then there was a much more lighthearted P.S. "The hair worked out brilliantly. You should consider opening your own salon!"

He read the letter two or three times, absorbing all the information its guarded language conveyed. Ellen was the woman they hadn't had time to visit on Mustique. Apparently she had been instrumental in helping Lucy disappear to Bequia and become Ruby. Clearly a trusted confidant, he guessed she knew as much as anybody about the events that put Lucy on the run. Maybe she had been involved in the latest disappearance as well. It was definitely worth a trip back to Mustique, even if it was just to talk to her.

The detection of this link made him tingle with the thrill of discovery. He wished he could be with Ingrid and Justine exploring the house in Friendship Bay, but he knew it was not safe for any of them. Instead he clicked on the Internet Explorer button and checked his email.

Another message from Amelia Brookstone awaited him.

"Glad to hear you have settled in with Lucy's pals. She wrote me that they were a good lot. Have you checked out the Apoplexica angle yet? It is hard to imagine Lu falling in with them; that type doesn't appeal to me, you never know what they might be into what with drugs, kinky tattoos, etc. But then Lulu and I always were very different. She always trusted people I would never trust. Be careful, Tyler."

Perhaps Tyler was just in an analytical frame of mind, but the tone of this email was not the same as Amelia's previous ones. It was more intimate, confiding her personal preferences. And then there was the way she referred to "the Apoplexica angle." He couldn't imagine that phrase coming out of Amelia's proper British mouth. She must be watching too many detective shows on the telly.

Logging out of his mail account, he did a quick search through the history of sites visited in the last few weeks but nothing stood out as unusual or suspicious. With a few guilt–ridden key strokes he tried to access Ingrid's email but that was indeed password protected.

As he waited for the computer to shut itself down, he stared out the open door. Just a glimpse of the turquoise sea was visible through the dense foliage around the village buildings. He had to think like Lucy. If he was Lucy and he needed to go somewhere safe with his child, where would he go? He would probably want to put as many miles as he could between himself and whatever the danger was, travel to the opposite side of the earth.

Although sometimes the safest place to hide was right under the nose of the pursuer. It had obviously worked for Lucy for nearly three years. Until it had stopped working.

Shutting the back door of the school behind him, he stepped out into the late afternoon sunlight. From somewhere on the slope of the road above him he heard his name being shouted.

"Tyler, mon. I hear dere are two, tree, maybe four beers at De Reef waiting with our initials on dem." Calvin approached him rapidly and clapped a hand on Tyler's back in his usual boisterous manner.

Tyler responded with a similar gesture and a grin. "Yes, mon. You are so right. Because it's time to plan our return visit to Mustique."

CHAPTER 11

Someone was rapping on his head with a wooden bat and it sounded hollow and empty inside except for the sound of his name echoing over and over again. Tyler opened his eyes and, in the excruciating brightness of the morning, realized that it was not his head but the door that Justine was banging on, quietly calling his name to wake him up.

"You not to get so hung over when there's work to be done, mon!" she scolded him none too gently.

"Blame that brother of yours!" he groaned back. "He's the one that kept me out partying until all hours."

Feeling around on Ingrid's side of the bed, he tried to remember whether she had been there in the night. He seemed to recall her coming in even later than he had, but that was all.

"Where's Ingrid? What happened with her?" The inside of his mouth was as dry as dust; his tongue felt like a salami.

"She gone before sunrise. Off sailing to Mustique. Just as we planned. Now get your lazy ass out of bed! Coffee is ready."

Off as planned. The buoyant feeling of accomplishment had him on his feet and into the shower sooner than was usual with a hangover. With his wet hair slicked back and sunglasses on, sipping hot coffee on the deck, he could almost pretend he felt fine. "So what did she say, did you talk to her?"

Justine shook her head as she bent intently over the toenails she was painting a vivid shade of pink. "All she say was, 'I'm off to Mustique with the band, see you tomorrow.' Or maybe she said 'with the Sands'. Or maybe she said 'with Sands in my hand'. Get over it, boy! Have some patience."

Tyler found that his imagination easily projected from Ingrid dancing and drinking with the Irish band members to Ingrid topless on a sailboat, French–kissing a nameless someone...a man or woman, it was hard to decide. He wondered for a minute just how much he cared what Ingrid did this weekend; they had no real commitment to each other, just an intense sexual connection. Would it matter to him if she had mindless sex in the heat of the moment or for the sake of the mission? The fact that he was detached enough to even consider the issue was a sufficient answer to the question.

The sound of footsteps on the stairs announced Calvin's arrival. His beaming face seemed to deny any trace of a hangover fog. "Tyler, mon. Word in de village is – " he paused for effect on the top step – "they know who is de body."

Tyler stared at him blankly. "What body?"

"The one they find in Friendship Bay. They say it is some drug–running captain from some place near Venezuela. And not just drugs him carry. Some say him deal in any kind of contraband." Calvin disappeared into the open door and could be heard helping himself to coffee.

Musing silently on this news, Tyler wondered if there was any connection to Apoplexica. "What about his boat?" He called after Calvin. "Did they find it?"

"No one say anyt'ing about him boat. Guess I have more work to do, ey, Mr. Investigator?" Calvin reappeared, grinning, his mouth full of banana, and tossed the peel into the thick underbrush over the edge of the deck.

"Yeah, see what you can find out about the boat. And speaking of boats – did you see if Derek is free tomorrow for a trip to Mustique?"

Calvin shook his head. "No, him gone already fishing early dis morning. I let you know tonight."

Tyler's head began to pound, this time just from thinking. This was all more complicated than anything he had done in years. It would be easier to stop now and not go on. But he knew he had to prohibit himself from that kind of backsliding. He would just face the task at hand today, go one step at a time.

Grimacing, he realized that was the philosophy that all addicts used to face their daily lives.

"Cecily, this is a friend of mine who is going to help me take some measurements for painting."

Tyler bent down to shake Cecily's gnarled brown hand, wondering if the tiny woman knew enough island gossip to be aware of who he was. "Very pleased to meet you," she murmured in a soft, raspy voice. "I will be changing the bed sheets upstairs if you have any questions."

Cecily backed away from Justine and Tyler without looking up, a wraith in a loose blue dress with a halo of wispy gray angel hair. She reminded him of some of the old women he knew on Grenada, dear ancient souls with bright eyes and merry laughs, who fussed over him in a grandmotherly way.

They were in the cavernous foyer of the monstrous mansion. Unfurnished, with a marble floor and a twenty foot ceiling that spanned the height of the entire house, it was an echo chamber for even the smallest whisper. Putting her finger to her lips, Justine led him towards the back of the house where a long open kitchen/dining area spanned the length of the building. Equipped with steel appliances and black Plexiglas counters and stools, it was the antithesis of any other décor Tyler had seen on Bequia. One wall of the room was entirely windows that overlooked the craggy, uncultivated hillside behind the estate.

"Here's the first thing they want me to paint." Justine pointed out a white dividing wall that separated the cooking and eating areas. She lowered her voice. "In a few minutes I will show you the lower level. I think you might find it interesting. And the best part," she spoke loudly again, "is the cupola on top of the house with a view of the entire Friendship Bay."

From deep within the recesses of her canvas tote of art supplies she withdrew a retractable tape measure and a notepad. Placing them in Tyler's hands, she said, "The tools of your trade. Now make yourself look busy."

Because there was so little in the way of furniture, it did not take long to scan the middle level of the house. Besides the kitchen, there was an enormous living room with a sound system designed to fill the size of the space. Other than a couple of leather couches and a coffee table full of ashtrays, there were few personal touches except for a massive collection of CD's and a couple of magazines. It didn't seem like this crew did much more than listen to music and smoke cigarettes. Tyler was surprised there was no big screen TV, but perhaps that was in another room.

In his peripheral vision he caught sight of Cecily coming down the stairs carrying a basket full of laundry. "Here, let me get that for you," he offered, moving quickly to relieve her of the load. "Which way is the laundry room?"

"What a nice young mon," she remarked, giving him the points he had hoped to score. "Most of dem here not be helpin' me a'tall. Machine is down below, dis way."

She led the way down a carpeted set of stairs to the next level of the hillside house and then down one more set of wooden stairs to a much cooler basement area carved out of the foundation rocks. There were no windows in this area and only the most primitive of finishing had been done. While Cecily filled the machine with dirty sheets, Tyler did a quick 360 degree scan and was surprised to see a wooden door in the wall behind him. It stood halfway open, enough for him to take a few steps sideways and peek inside.

The fluorescent light spilling over from the laundry area was enough for him to see that the door led to some sort of storage room. Wide wooden shelves three feet apart lined the walls and a vent in the ceiling indicated some sort of ventilation system. Tyler was not sure what it reminded him of; in Vermont it would have been a root cellar, in his early childhood on Long Island it might have been a home fallout shelter. Maybe it was simply for storing stuff, but the isolated and protected location caused him to believe otherwise.

"Cecily, do you have any other loads you'd like me to help you carry down?" Tyler was back at her side by the time the wash had started.

"You are too good for dis place," she scolded him. "Yes, if you want to help, come. But don't let me keep you from your own work."

"I have all day," he assured her as they started back up the stairs. "It's no problem. So, have you lived on Bequia all your life?"

As he had imagined, she was happy to talk about her long life on the island and all the people she had known or heard about. In her 74 years she had seen the island go from a whaling community to a tourist–based economy and she did not seem sorry to see the old ways left behind. "I like my TV," she laughed. "TV not run on whale oil, you know."

Cautiously he asked her if she knew the Sunny Island School in Lower Bay and if she had ever met a friend of his, a short blonde woman named Ruby who worked there. Cecily did indeed remember seeing her, buying tomatoes in the market and at church a few times. Tyler didn't reveal his astonishment at that news, but he supposed after what Lucy had been through she might have felt like saying a few prayers.

"Did you ever see her visiting here with the band?"

Cecily shook her head. "But then, I am not here at night, only in the daylight hours. Some time, before the wifes arrive, they have all kind party here. I know because I have to clean up the next morning."

"Parties? With who? Local people or friends from abroad?"

"Me never see it, you know, but me hear it from some local girls, a few boys what sell de ganja, some white tourists." Cecily lowered her voice. "I don't care, you know. I work for dem, dey pay me and dat is where de arrangement end. Now let me ax you, have you seen de view from de top?"

Moments later he was standing in the cupola on top of the house. With glass walls on all four sides, the view encompassed the entire bay as well as the road to the top of the hill. The cloudless sky was clear enough to afford a vista across the sea beyond Petit Nevis and as far as Mustique. He could see a handful of yachts bobbing in the calm shallow waters, but nothing that matched the number of vessels on the other side of the island in Admiralty Bay.

He wondered if these boats had cleared customs before sailing around Bequia to anchor in Friendship Bay. Chances were slim that they had bothered to let the immigration office know they were here. Who would know? In fact, who would know much about anything that happened on the back side of this island?

It was the perfect scenario for any smuggling operation. There was no question in his mind now that this vantage point on the roof had everything to do with the storage room in the basement.

Although Tyler was looking at the sea, out of the corner of his eye he sensed movement on the road behind him and turned in time to see a taxi making its way down the hill. He was surprised to see it make the hairpin turn into the steep driveway below.

By pressing his face to the window, he could just make out what was happening directly beneath his crow's nest position. A man and a woman were climbing out of the open back of the taxi; they stepped aside to wait while the driver retrieved their luggage. From his high vantage point, Tyler could not make out their faces, but he could see that the man had his graying blond hair pulled back in a long thin ponytail and the woman had a spiky do in an improbable shade of blue, the style being similar to Justine's drawing of Eileen Sands.

As the vehicle backed out into the road, the man shaded his face and looked up at the enormity of the house. Something about his stance was familiar, and although Tyler couldn't place it, he had a bad feeling all the same. He considered hiding out in the cupola as long as he could, but then he realized their suitcases indicated that this was more than just a drive–by visit. As he climbed down the steep steps he could hear the doorbell ringing. By the time he reached the stairs to the first floor, Cecily had answered it and was explaining to the couple that the residents were all on their way to Mustique for the weekend.

A string of four letter words mixed with profanities known only in the British Isles stopped Tyler in his tracks. It was not the foul language that made his knees buckle, it was the voice articulating it. The intonation had a unique and recognizable quality to it, like glass breaking on gravel, mixed with cigar smoke. He leaned against the cool cement wall and closed his eyes, trying to remember and forget at the same time. Was it back in a pub on the outskirts of London, or had it been seconds before he was pushed off a curb in a front of a bus?

Like a small child, he sank down on the steps and watched the scene below unfolding. "Can't fookin' believe they lef' without us...one bloody hour of delay at Heathrow and look what fookin' happens...he knew we were fookin' comin'..."

Like a vibrant angel of tolerance wearing colorful island clothing, Justine floated in from the kitchen to rescue Cecily from his livid tirade. "Sounds like you two missed the boat," she said in a jolly tone. "Literally."

"Our plane was delayed in London yesterday," the woman explained, glaring at her companion. "We missed the last flight from Barbados and had to spend the night there. We didn't realize they would be leaving this early for Mustique."

"The bloody plane was on its way to fookin' Mustique after it dropped us off here," the man shouted, kicking one of the suitcases. "We could've just flown there!"

"Welcome to Bequia." Justine extended her hand and spoke softly and calmly, displaying the perfect antithesis to his lack of control. "I'm Justine, the house muralist. We have a lovely island here and I'm sure once you have a shower and a bite to eat, you can go down to the beach and feel much better about being on Bequia."

It was the woman who accepted Justine's hand. "Claire O'Shea. And this is my husband, Brian. He's the band manager. Sorry about his behavior; the whole trip has been a bit trying."

"Cecily, is there a room ready for these tired travelers?" Justine was the model of hospitality, even in a house that wasn't hers.

"Yes, mon, of course. Jus' follow me." Before Tyler had a chance to stumble to his feet, Cecily was leading all of them up the stairs. Standing quickly, he tried to flash a warning glance at Justine, who he knew would be compelled by her good manners to introduce him immediately.

"And this is my co–worker–"

"Mack. Mackie Tyburn. Let me give you a hand with that." He took a heavy suitcase from Claire O'Shea and turned away quickly.

But Brian was already frowning. "Mackie Tyburn, you say? You remind me of someone, can't bloody think of who. Ever been to Great Britain?"

Tyler shook his head and hoped the sweat dripping down the back of his neck would be attributed to the heat of the day and the weight of the luggage. "Nope, I'm a local islander. Came here on a yacht twenty some years ago and loved it so much I never left."

"Then you're not really local," Claire giggled. "Where are you from originally?"

"San Diego, California. My father worked at the shipyard there. Been involved with the sea one way or another all my life. Here you go." Tyler relieved himself of the suitcase inside the guest bedroom door and turned to Justine. "Gotta go, baby." As she squinted her eyes suspiciously, he leaned over and gave her a kiss on the cheek. "I'm late to meet Calvin. Walk me to the door."

Wrapping his arm lovingly around her and guiding her towards the stairs, he called over his shoulder, "Nice to meet you both."

"What the hell is going on, Tyler?" she hissed quietly at him once they were out of earshot. "What was that all about?"

"What do you think? I hate to leave you on your own but I have to get out of here." He handed her the tape measure and notepad.

"Tyler, be straight with me. Does he really know you from somewhere?"

He leaned forward and whispered in her ear. "Well, he tried to kill me a couple of times. Does that count as knowing me?"

For the first time since he'd met her, he saw Justine's composure slip away for a split second. "What should I say if he asks me about you? He's must think I am your girlfriend."

Tyler opened the door and stepped outside, pulling Justine with him. "I know it's not in your nature, but I need you to lie your head off. Say whatever you have to. Just don't tell him where I live. We live." He squeezed her hand and gave her a shaky grin. "See you tonight, girlfriend."

He tried not to run down the driveway. He needed to find Calvin right away. If there was ever a time to get off the island for a day, it was now.

CHAPTER TWELVE

It was nearly noon the next day by the time Tyler and Calvin stood outside the small turquoise wooden house situated alone at the edge of the main village on Mustique. They had waited nearly two hours for Derek to show up at the dock in Paget Farm. When he finally arrived, he announced that he wanted to be back in Bequia by three because he heard that the Apoplexica band members and possibly Kip Kingsley were going to show up at De Reef for the Sunday afternoon party. That only gave Tyler a little more than an hour to call on Ellen and win her trust enough to confide in him.

As they contemplated the neat traditional cottage and its dirt yard, the gleeful sound of children's voices could be heard approaching on the road behind them. Turning, they saw a colorful entourage moving in their direction; girls dressed in their pastel Sunday best with hats and gloves, boys uncomfortable in shirts and ties, and the woman who towered over them, her bountiful figure covered by yards of lavender floral print fabric. As her features came into view, Tyler saw that she was a strikingly handsome woman with a face defined by a high forehead, angular cheekbones and full lips.

"Into de house, all of you, and take de church clothes off ri' now!" she ordered in a tone that commanded authority but with a pleasant timber. She turned to face the two strangers in her dooryard. "And what can I do for you gentlemen?"

"Ellen?" Tyler extended his hand. "I'm an old friend of Lucy Brookstone's. I think you are too."

Ellen stared in horror at his hand as if it were a weapon of mass destruction rather than a gesture of friendship. "Who are you?" In a matter of seconds, her sweet voice had become a harsh whisper.

"Tyler Mackenzie. I'm sure Lucy must have mentioned me to you. She and I lived together for a few years before she hooked up with Kip."

The tight lines in Ellen's face softened a bit and she peered intensely at Tyler's face. "Yes," she said after a moment. "She did talk about you. Where you been all dis time?"

It was not the response Tyler had expected and he stumbled a bit over his reply. "In– in – Grenada. Not very far away. Why?"

"Grenada? No! You tellin' me just dat far? A few small islands from here?" She shook her head and passed a hand across her eyes before looking up again, this time accusingly. "She not here anymore, you know."

"Yes, I know. Her sister contacted me; I've been on Bequia. Look, would you mind if we came inside and talked to you for a few minutes?"

There was an awkward silence. Then Ellen opened the door to the house and led them inside to a small front room crowded with furnishings. A china cupboard with glass doors seemed to dominate the two straight–backed wooden chairs that were jammed in on other side of a wicker settee with chintz cushions. A tiny portable television sat on a small wooden pedestal table next to the door.

Ellen sat on the settee while Calvin and Tyler settled themselves uncomfortably on the chairs. From the back of the house the excited chatter of children came through the curtained doorway that separated the rooms. "You mind you not t'row de clothes on de floor now!" Ellen shouted sternly.

"Are all those children yours?" Tyler asked politely.

"Most. A few dat I care for belong to my sister who living in Toronto, Canada. Since I not working for Mr. Kingsley, she been sending us money to help out wit' de expense. I care for some white children during de tourist season but it not pay de bills all year long. So you seen her?" she asked without any more formalities.

"Lucy? No, she's disappeared. That's why we're here. We thought maybe you might have some idea where she might have gone."

"Disappeared? She not on Bequia any longer? But—" she seemed somewhat disconcerted by the idea.

"We think it's because Kip Kingsley started going there and that his friends in the band, Apoplexica, bought a house on the island," Tyler explained gently.

There was no mistaking the look of alarm that passed across her face.

"Ellen, you're the only one who can help us," Tyler went on.

"What do you mean?" She frowned at him and crossed her arms defensively. "Why is that?"

" I know she was close to you. I found a draft of the letter she sent you after she left Mustique. Apparently you helped her transform herself into Ruby." Tyler watched as Ellen sighed and plucked at a loose piece of wicker on the arm of the settee. "Her sister has hired me to find her; did Lucy ever tell you I use to do this kind of work? I was hoping you could shed some light on just exactly why she left Mustique for Bequia."

"And what exactly are you going to do with the information if I tell it to you?" Ellen's eyes flashed indignantly and her body stiffened.

"You can trust him," Calvin assured her. "He is on Ruby's side, I mean, Lucy's."

Ellen looked at Calvin as if seeing him for the first time. "And who are you?"

"I was her best friend on Bequia." Calvin flashed his inimitable smile. "I love her as much as dis man here."

Calvin's statement of the truth made them all so uncomfortable that the awkward laughter that followed broke the tension in the room. "All right then. So we are three people who love dis woman. What do you t'ink I can tell you dat might be important now?"

Tyler relaxed a little now that it seemed as if Ellen could be won over. "Well, I was hoping you might be able to tell me why she ran from Mustique in the first place. And why only as far as Bequia."

Ellen sighed. "Why you t'ink she ran? Dat man, Kingsley. Dat bastard."

"So their relationship wasn't good then?" Tyler hoped he hadn't spoken those words with too much satisfaction.

" Wasn't good? Ha." Ellen spat in her hand. "No, de mon not treat her well after de boy was born. T'ings change wit children, you know."

"How long did you work for Kingsley?"

"Nine years, mon. Nine years and it over like nothing. De mon a true bastard." Ellen shook her head and murmured what sounded like prayers under her breath.

" And why exactly did he fire you?"

"It a long story. But basically he not like my friendship wit' Lucy." Ellen settled herself into the cushions of the settee and removed the church–going hat she still had on her head. "But de trouble between dem, it started after Tucker was born. You know Tucker."

"Well, I've never met him but–"

"I know Mr. T," Calvin chimed in. "We were good friends."

"So I work for Mr. Kingsley long enough to know him tastes not so natural. I know him before Miss Lucy ever show her face on Mustique and him have some different kine' girlfriend before her, you know. Everyone t'ink dat everyt'ing change for him wit' a wife and chile, but it not really so. Even while she pregnant, him have other women around." Ellen shook her head in disapproval.

"What was different after Tucker was born?" Tyler asked.

He was surprised to see Ellen's cheeks suddenly grow quite pink. "He become obsessed," she said quietly.

"Obsessed?"

"Yes, wit' de change in Lucy's titties."

Neither Tyler nor Calvin knew how to respond to that unexpected statement. Tyler cleared his throat abruptly. "And just how was Kip obsessed?"

Ellen giggled uneasily. "Dis is not easy for me to talk about, you know. Me never tell any living person dis."

"But you can tell us," Tyler assured her warmly. "Because we are here to help Lucy."

"Him love de idea her titties grow so big and full of milk. And hers grow so much bigger den some. He want dem always to stay dat way. He order some special machine dat take de milk when de baby don' want it. We never see such a t'ing down here before." Ellen shook her head, still disbelieving.

Tyler could feel the sweat rolling down the back of his neck. He really didn't want to know any of this information, but he listened anyway knowing it might have some relevance.

"Even after Tucker him not interested in de titty anymore, Mr. Kingsley he keep after Lucy to use de machine to keep de breasts big and de milk flowing. It not make any sense but he was very...strong about how him felt. He —" Tears filled her eyes and she looked at the floor. "He did mean t'ings, bad t'ings to her," she whispered. "He not treat her right anymore."

On one side of his peripheral vision, Tyler could see Calvin's hands curling into fists and uncurling over and over again. "What about the boy? How did Kingsley feel about him?"

"He not know what to do wit' a child." From somewhere in the recesses of her dress, Ellen produced a handkerchief and dabbed with it at her eyes. "Any time de baby cry or fuss, he not want anyt'ing to do wit' it. De man too old for small children. Only children him like is de girls whose body grow up too fast."

"He ever hurt dat boy?" Calvin asked darkly.

"He never strike him, if dat what you mean. But he hurt him plenty wit' his words and actions."

For a moment they all sat in silence, each of them dealing with their own personal reactions to Ellen's revelations. "I don't understand why Lucy would put up with all of that," Tyler said finally. "Why didn't she leave sooner?"

"It no so easy as you might t'ink. She pretty much a prisoner of dat place and to leave wit' a small child is no easy t'ing."

" A prisoner?" he repeated slowly.

Ellen nodded. "Yes, truly. He keep de gates locked and when she allowed to go out sometimes to take de baby to de beach, he make Rudy go wit' dem. If you axed him, Kingsley, him would say he trying to keep dem safe from kidnappers and all, dat Rudy was dey bodyguard, dat be him twisted story de whole time. But after some time, he go to do him music business in England and he leave dem here for months alone. No one allowed to visit, none of de big party like when himself here, and de only ones can come in de gate are us who work for him."

It was a depressing picture she was painting of Lucy's glamorous life as a rock star's wife on Mustique. Tyler felt an intense pain in his chest and knew it was the overwhelming sadness of learning what Lucy, the independent firebrand, had been forced to endure. The air in the little house suddenly seemed stale and oppressive. "So what happened in the end? How did she finally escape?"

Ellen's eyes flashed with anger now. "He took her passport, you know, so she couldn't leave de island. And he made sure she have no money. But none of dat would have stopped her. Tucker was what kept her there. She try a couple times to borrow money from some of Kingsley's friends when dey visit, but him find out and he punish her." She hung her head, clearly not wanting to talk about it. As much as he wanted to know the horrifying details, Tyler did not ask.

"But you helped her."

"Yes. I was the only one of de household who showed her any kindness, even though him warn me against doing so. De final t'ing happen at a party – Kingsley was leaving for a music tour and he was having himself a going–away fete. Me never sure what exactly de cause of him anger dis time, but de next day Rudy show up at me house wit' Tucker and say Kingsley want me to keep him here until him say so and not to go up to de house again." Tears rolled freely down her dark cheeks now. "He knew it was de worse t'ing he could do to Lucy, dat why he do it."

Calvin, who had been swearing softly during Ellen's story, could not control himself any longer. "De man EVIL!" He spat the words out as though they tasted foul.

Ellen nodded vigorously. "Yes, mon. Evil is de word. I knew him would make sure Lucy not know where Tucker was or if him safe, so I managed to sneak her a message wit' my brother who make food deliveries up dat way. Den I work out a plan wit' my brother to help her escape de place." She sat up straighter suddenly and looked at them sternly as if they were small children. "Now you mus' promise dat no one will ever know what I am going to tell you now, or my brother and me, we can both go to jail."

Tyler and Calvin both assured her that they were on her side. "So how did you get her out of there?"

"My brother distract Rudy at de gate while Lucy climb out around de back by de pool. It possible to climb over onto de cliff and a little track run beyond the walls."

Tyler nodded; it was the same way he had gotten into Kip's house.

" It was just nightfall which gave Lucy a good chance dat it would be morning before Rudy discover her gone. Dey come down here to my house where I cut and color her hair. First t'ing at dawn, she and Tucker are on a little speedboat to Bequia. It seem like de best place to send her at de moment since she have no passport and de two islands really not do much business wit' each other. She have a little bit of money and an old credit card of her own dat Kip not know of. And I give her de money Kip lef' me to care for Tucker."

"And what happened when Rudy realized she was missing?"

"What you t'ink, mon? He come running down to see if she was hiding here. He search de house and tear it up. He rough me up a little too." Ellen dashed away a stray tear. "Lucky for me, he t'inking Tucker gone to school with de other children; him too stupid to know Tucker too young for school. Him come again in de evening and by den my brother is back and can help me against him. I tell Rudy dat Tucker never come home from school, dat Lucy must have taken him from there after she escape. After a while, dey have de whole police force search all of Mustique for her, but dey never find no clues."

"And what about Kip? How did he take it?"

"Him not come back to de island for some time after dat so he must not care too much. When him do finally come back, him have a new girlfriend wit' him and shortly after she leave, he take up wit' his local woman friend, Jadene, again."

What had happened to the picture–book romance that Lucy had described to him back in London? Somewhere along the line, something had gone terribly wrong. "And when was the last time you heard from Lucy?"

"Not long after she arrive on Bequia she send me a letter telling me dey are safe. It the last I ever hear from her. And now you telling me she gone again?"

"Yes, as of a few months ago. She probably was able to get herself a new passport so she could be anywhere this time. Did she ever talk to you about some place she might want to go?"

Ellen shook her head. "We never even talk about Bequia until a few hours before she leave. My brother t'ink it up as de right place. It seem Lucy just t'ink she stay wit' me and hide but we know dat can't happen."

Their time was almost up and Calvin and Tyler thanked Ellen profusely for sharing her story with them. "There's just one last thing," Tyler said as he stood up. "Did she ever talk about the band, Apoplexica?"

At the mention of Apoplexica, Ellen let out a string of swear words that would have astounded her church–going associates. "Those rude boys. She not have to talk about dem, I know dem myself, having to pick up garbage after dey have spent all night t'rowing it around de house and pool, never a nice word from dem to me ever, dey treat me worse den de dirt under their feet. No, it never a good day when Apoplexica come to visit on Mustique."

"So Lucy saw them fairly regularly then?" Tyler was trying hard to puzzle this relationship out.

"Whenever dey show up, once or twice a year, but after de baby born, she not party very much anymore. She stay away, closed up at de other end of de house. She probably not have much to do wit' dem."

"She never talked to you about them?"

"Not specifically, no. A lot of dat type come to Kingsleys; dey not anyt'ing special. I know she try to keep de baby away from de drugs and all. And she try to stay away from de sex activities." Ellen whispered the last few words.

Tyler had seen a lot of things in his lifetime, and right now he did not want to dwell on what went on at Kip Kingsley's estate. Perhaps Ingrid would fill him in later, but maybe he did not even want to know. "Ellen, thank you so much," he said again. "When I finally catch up with Lucy, I will make sure she gets in touch with you somehow. And if you think of anything else that might be important —" he stopped and scribbled Ingrid's phone number on a piece of paper — "call me and let me know."

Ellen touched his arm at the door. "You must find her," she told him in a quiet insistent voice. "She needs you to find dem."

"Why do you t'ink she say dat?" Calvin asked him as they walked down the road back towards the dock. Of all the things that they had heard, it was the easiest thing to talk about.

Tyler didn't know; all he knew was that it made him feel a little bit uncomfortable. And very confused. "Let's stop and get some beers for the trip back," he suggested. "Maybe that'll help us make sense of all this."

CHAPTER THIRTEEN

By the time Calvin and Tyler staggered ashore the beach at Lower Bay they were already fairly intoxicated. Consequently they fit right in with the crowd growing around De Reef. They were just two more glassy–eyed drinkers, who went pretty much unnoticed as they made their way between the soccer players on the sand and the Sunday party–goers hanging around the edges of the beach bar.

"It nearly de Christmas, you know," Calvin remarked. "It getting busier and busier from now till Old Year's Night."

Tyler had no idea what the date was, but as he tried to puzzle it out in his fogged brain, it seemed like Christmas must be any day now. Not that it mattered; he hadn't celebrated it in all the years he'd been on Grenada. Caribbean people didn't make the same big deal of the holidays that Americans and Brits did, at least not in the material, gift–giving sense. They partied hard on Boxing Day, the day after Christmas, and there was always a New Year's celebration, but the decorating and ostentatious materialism he had grown up with did not, and clearly could not, exist in the Third World.

"Look dere, at de yacht to de right, mon." Calvin touched Tyler's arm and pointed." See, it be Ingrid, climbing into de dinghy to come ashore."

Peering out to sea where Calvin indicated, Tyler was just in time to see someone on board toss Ingrid her bikini top and the postures of everyone in the rubber boat as they laughed hysterically.

"Look like she havin' she–self a good time," Calvin remarked.

"Too good." Tyler wasn't even sure what he meant by his response or how he felt about it. "Who she with?"

"Look like de Apoplexia people. But me not sure what Kingsley look like these days. But when I do see him, I want to bash his fuckin' evil face in, mon."

"Calvin–" Tyler turned to him in alarm." You can't do it, man. You're not supposed to know about any of it. You have to control yourself. We'll get back at him, I promise you, but not yet. You can't show your hand yet."

A deep frown creased Calvin's normally smooth brow." It going to be hard, but I will try to control myself."

"Try isn't good enough. You MUST not touch the man." They were startled by a loud chord of music followed by a drum roll." Sounds like Kip may already be here. Let's get inside."

Squeezing their way between two middle–aged fleshy couples with skin the color of boiled lobsters, Tyler and Calvin found a vantage point from which they could watch both the stage and the beach. Sure enough, a white–haired Kip Kingsley and his electric guitar were plugged in next to a bald, well–muscled bongo player and an androgynous female saxophone player, transforming the usual laid–back island sound into something more metallic.

Despite his newfound hatred for the musician, Calvin could not keep himself from beaming with delight at the wonder of a celebrity performance in Lower Bay. The local crowd was responding in a wild and enthusiastic way, unprecedented by anything Tyler had seen so far in Bequia." I'll get us some drinks before it gets too crazy," he shouted at Calvin, who nodded and smiled without hearing a word he'd said.

In the several minutes it took Tyler to make his way to the bar and then wait his turn three–deep for the bartender, Ingrid and her friends had managed to wriggle their way under the roof of De Reef and get closer to the bar then he had. As a result he suddenly found himself elbow to elbow with Ingrid waiting for a chance to order drinks.

"Haven't I seen you somewhere before?" he asked looking at her sideways.

"Don't look at me," she murmured staring straight ahead. "We don't know each other."

"Any man of sound sexual health would look at you," Tyler laughed." It would seem more unnatural if I didn't notice you."

"Okay, then, no you haven't seen me anywhere before and I don't want to know you." She still wouldn't meet his gaze.

"Everything fine with you?" Tyler looked down and rummaged with the change in his pocket.

"Fine. Moses, I need three gin and tonics, three Heinekens and a white wine."

"Good time last night?"

She was still not looking at him, but he could see the ghost of her dimples as she suppressed a smile." I'm a free–spirited Swede; I always have a good time." Beneath the bar, she pressed her knee against his.

"Ingrid, luv, add a rum punch!" a British accent bellowed from behind.

"Right–o, Ethan!" she called over her shoulder. "I'm with friends, buddy, so another time." Looking the other direction, she continued the pressure against his leg.

"Right–o, then," Tyler replied mockingly. "Moses, give me six Hairouns." He figured three beers a piece should hold Calvin and himself for at least an hour.

Cradling the ice cold bottles against his chest, he maneuvered his way to the edge of the open building where the concrete floor dropped off to the soft sand of the beach. It was less claustrophobic on the perimeter of the crowd, although it was harder to keep his eye on Ingrid and her pals. Amazingly Calvin materialized at his shoulder to relieve him of half the beers. Stuffing one in each of the pockets of his shorts and downing most of the third, he was gone again, disappearing into the pulsing throng that surrounded the stage.

Luckily, Tyler was tall enough to see over most heads and now he saw that the local celebrities and their friends had managed to get a couple of tables front and center. He ran his eyes and his memory over each of their faces, trying to fit them all into their places in the present and past.

There was Ethan Sands and his wife, Eileen, looking like they'd had something more to enhance their moods besides mere alcohol. The skin–head drummer and the bass player with the pierced tongue, both of whom he recognized but whose names he couldn't remember, were there with their respective women. One was too fat and flabby to look attractive in the string bikini she sported, the other was all bones with a sour pinched face.

The wife of Brian, the road manager, sat next to those two, trying unsuccessfully to have a conversation with them. Brian himself appeared decidedly on edge, still wearing his sunglasses even in the shade of the building, apparently on the lookout for someone or something. On the other side of the table, the statuesque black woman with the elegant long neck and pouting lips had to be the infamous Jadene; he didn't recognize the two island women with her, but they were clearly just hangers–on.

It was hard to tell where Brian's gaze, hidden behind dark glasses, was resting and Tyler began to feel uncomfortably conspicuous. He watched as Ingrid arrived with the drinks and squeezed herself between the drummer and bass player, who both put their arms around her to keep her from falling between the chairs. The three of them tossed their heads back and laughed at something funny she said and then he saw Brian lean forward and ask her a question, nodding in Tyler's direction. With a cursory look at him, she shook her

148

head and then purposefully leaned forward to kiss the skin–head man on her right.

Tyler turned his back on them and looked out to sea. A dark bulky shape he recognized as Rudy was descending into the rubber dinghy moored by Kingsley's yacht where three women in bright t–shirts waited expectantly. As they motored into shore, Tyler wondered if there was anyone still on board. He was not sure what secrets the empty boat might yield, but it was hard not to pass up an opportunity to find out.

"Hey." He turned towards the damp hand tapping his upper arm. A local man with a red bandana tied around his head was holding out a beer to him." De mon in de shades at de table up front sent dis to you."

Tyler glanced quickly over at Ingrid's table to see Brian raise a forefinger and nod. Tyler tipped the beer at him in thanks and upended it. He was unsure of what the friendly overture indicated, but he wasn't going to ignore it. Edging his way to the steps leading down to the beach, he joined the small crowd that was enjoying the sight of Rudy trying to drag the little boat up onto the shore so that the three women passengers could step out onto the sand without getting wet.

"Watch me silk pants!" one cried and the others shrieked with laughter as she backed over the edge, her oversized behind and thighs gleaming in their shiny purple splendor. They roared again as her high–heeled sandals sunk into the sand like golf tees.

With all eyes on this spectacle of inappropriate dress, Tyler slipped unnoticed into the water and began swimming away from the beach in the direction of the yacht.

Normally a strong, relaxed swimmer, he did not doubt his ability to reach his destination several hundred yards away. But he was only about halfway there when an inexplicable exhaustion began to push its way through his limbs, seeping into his muscles and clouding his brain. He flipped over onto his back to float for a bit, he thought maybe he just needed a little rest, just close his eyes for a few minutes and sleep...

He sputtered awake as water began filling his nose and mouth, and he forced his eyes open. His vision was blurry and out of focus, his mind was foggy, but he knew he had to find something to hold on to. The red and green hull of a water taxi seemed to be just a few feet away. He thought his arms and legs were working, but it felt like he was underwater, wait, he was underwater, sinking and floundering and all he wanted to do was sleep...

With all his energy, he propelled himself forward, it was only a few strokes more until he reached the ladder of Kip's yacht, only a few strokes more. He felt the coldness of metal, wrapped his fingers tightly around it and painstakingly hauled himself out of the water, flopping onto the deck like a dying fish.

Just a little nap, that was all he needed. He crawled on his belly towards the cabin, tumbling face forward down the stairs to the closed hatchway. He could not sleep here, someone would find him, he couldn't risk that...

Summoning up the last of his strength, he managed to pull the door open and stagger inside. Although unable to process the spaciousness of the interior, his numbed brain guided him towards a narrow hall. Through the first doorway on the left, a neatly made bed beckoned him to collapse into its comforting embrace.

Harsh raucous laughter penetrated the density of his deep slumber. For a few moments he could not figure out why his entire body was vibrating and then he realized that it was the reverberations of the boat's powerful motor. Shit, he thought dully, as his brain slowly worked through the meaning of where he was and what was happening. He carefully cracked his eyelids open, fearful of the daylight. The dusky illumination of his surroundings was not as painful as anticipated.

He was lying in a circle of clammy dampness and it crossed his mind briefly that he had wet the bed until he remembered dragging his body out of the water directly into somebody's fancy cabin on Kip Kingsley's extravagant yacht. Shivering in the humidity and closeness of the tiny room, he felt nauseous and thirsty and fearful of discovery. Was he a stowaway on a return voyage back to Mustique? The boat was too small for him to remain easily hidden.

Peals and shrieks of merriment in a familiar female timbre brought him closer to consciousness. At the groans of pleasure accompanied by a rhythmic thudding above his head, he forced his resistant muscles into a sitting position. Was he really listening to Ingrid screwing one of the band members on the other side of a fiberglass ceiling?

"Oh, fuck me, baby, fuck, fuck, fuck me..." a working–class British accent moaned and Tyler's stomach churned at the image of what was happening a few feet away.

"Oh, fuck me too, baby, me next," laughed another voice and Tyler squeezed his eyes shut again to block out what was now a double vision. His mind reeled with questions – What had happened to him that had made him pass out? How many others were on the boat? Where were they going? And what would they do when they found him?

Staying still was probably the best thing he could do for now. Through the open porthole at the head of the bed, he could hear grunting sounds reminiscent of wild boars mixed with breathless panting, punctuated by the wild orgasmic screams he knew so well. There was a silence broken with several wheezing gasps and then a slow thumping began again, accompanied by a different series of moans playing in counterpoint to Ingrid's increasingly louder cries of "Ja, ja, ja, JA, JA!"

Tyler realized he was literally biting his tongue — he had talked her into this, he knew that he was responsible for what he was being subjected to hearing, but he did not want to listen, he wanted it to stop, he could not think clearly at all.

The second round of sex was over much more quickly than the first and cigarette smoke was soon wafting through the air.

"Fucking awesome. Awesome fucking," a hoarse voice declared followed by a round of coughing.

"Best in a cunt's age," came the agreement. "Ingrid, you are one sweet piece of ass. Let's toss it again in a bit, what do you say?"

"Mmmm," was all he could hear of Ingrid's response.

"Think we wore her out, mate. Bitch is snoring like a sow. Nothing like a good three–way on deck at sunset, is there? Remember that time in St. Barts with that French chick?"

"Hey, talk about memories... Hey Brian, slow her down!" The motor slowed to a stuttering putter before shutting off completely. "Fucking shit, remember this place? What a near fuck–up last year."

"Christ almighty. I'll never forget. Moon fucking Hole, Ethan's dumb ass idea, almost did us in. Look at that stinkin' puny beach. What was he thinkin', dumb bastard."

Although, his head was growing heavy with the need to sleep again, Tyler inched closer to the porthole, straining to catch every word they said now.

"Aye. Well, no worries this year. Friendship Bay is as sweet a piece of cake as this pussy here. Oh, see me, I'm gettin' hard again just lookin' at her. God, she came like a volcano, didn't she?"

The two laughed again conspiratorily and Tyler felt vomit rising in his throat.

"Brian, Let's just swing over to Friendship for a bit. We've got a few more hours before we have to run her back to Lower Bay."

"What do you wankers think I am, your private fucking boat boy?" The motor started up again.

Tyler's weighty eyelids jerked open. There was another person on board and despite the slowness of his thinking processes, his brain matched the name with the voice. Brian, who had sent him the beer at De Reef – shit, it had probably been drugged with something and that was why he felt like this. What the hell was he going to do now…

His only option was to lay low and hope nobody came below deck and discovered him before they sailed back to De Reef. Despite his desperate effort to stay vigilant, the vibration of the motor lulled him back into the twilight zone of sleep.

When once again the engine cut off abruptly, he opened his eyes, unsure of whether five minutes or an hour had passed. The daylight was fading now and the semi–darkness gave him a false sense of security.

"This will probably be as close as they come to shore. Look up at the house – we can see the whole bay and all the way to Mustique from there."

"Yeah, but what I like best is our iron–clad alibi. Everybody on Bequia and their fuckin' cousin will be at De Reef and see us playing that New Year's Eve party all night."

"Good thing – we got twice as much shit passing through this time, coke, smack, tranks, burners choppers, nines. This shipment is the mother lode."

The smell of ganja smoke filled Tyler's nostrils now underscored by another round of uncontrollable coughing.

"Damn straight. Pass that thing here." A loud inhale was followed by more hacking. "Oh, that is good shit. Brian, you want some?"

Tyler tried to suppress the tickle rising in his own esophagus. He buried his face in the pillow and cleared his throat. What he wouldn't give for some water – maybe he could slip out into the galley and find something to drink. He crawled to the foot of the bed and peered through the door into the main part of the cabin.

Under cover of the clamoring footsteps overhead, he tried to slip silently out of the room. Already unsteady on his feet, a lurch of the boat threw him against a counter, sending a couple of empty beer bottles crashing to the floor.

Instantly a shadow appeared in the hatchway. "What the fuck–"

Tyler froze, hoping that he might be hidden in the dimness of the interior and then he was blinded by a sudden beam of bright light. "Well, look at the dog what the cat brought in." Brian's taunting voice came from somewhere behind the light and moved quickly towards him." Now put your hands where I can see them and don't move."

"You sound like a cheesy cop movie," Tyler said, or at least he thought he said, but all that came out of his mouth was a slurry of raspy and unintelligible whispers.

"Ha, I don't know how you are even still standing at this point," Brian sneered and with what seemed like a lightning fast move, but probably was not, he punched Tyler in the side of the head. As he collapsed to the floor, his skull banged against the edge of the wooden counter and he fell into a deep well of unconsciousness.

"Nobody, nobody..." His sense of sound rose to the surface before the rest of his senses. Pain was the next sensation he had – pounding and screeching through his forehead and face.

"No bodies – we can't have any bodies, there can be no trail, you know what I'm talking about." The words came more clearly now.

"So what the fuck are we going to do? Shit, I wish I wasn't so freakin' stoned. I can't think straight."

Despite the nauseating feeling that he was on the most–dizzying carnival ride of his life, Tyler managed to stay still and keep his eyes closed.

"Lenny, calm yourself down. Here's what is going to happen. You and Gustav are going to wake up your succulent slut and get into the dinghy and take her to shore. You will take her up to the house and Gustav, you are going to row back to the boat here and then you are going to take care of this 'nobody' here."

Tyler couldn't help himself – an involuntary shudder made all his limbs twitch." He's comin' to, Brian. What do we do?" Lenny sounded on the verge of tears.

"I told you, go put your friggin' pants on and get that slutty bitch off this yacht. Take her home and get her to suck you off since your dick has gone so limp, you chicken shit." Brian's voice was suddenly in Tyler's ear and he could feel his breath against his face. "You awake again, pretty boy?" Brian grabbed him by the jaw and twisted his head painfully upward, forcing his fingers into Tyler's mouth. "Maybe this will help you sleep more soundly."

Before he realized what was happening, a bottle was forced into his lips and he was gagging on the liquid being poured down his throat. He tried to sit up, but someone was sitting on his chest. Gagging and spewing from his nose and mouth, he passed out again.

It was the sound of his own moaning that woke him from a tortured and nightmarish sleep. He did not understand why his whole body seemed to be rocking back and forth or why his head felt like it was being jack–hammered, but he did know that he was going to be sick. He cracked his eyelids slightly so that he would not be blinded by the morning light but he was surrounded by darkness and it was not a velvety,

155

friendly darkness, rather an unfamiliar swirling black hole.

Eyes wide open now, he struggled to sit up. His hands came into contact with the sticky plastic surface of the alien cushion beneath him and his head whacked hard into something directly above. The sudden blow to his skull brought his nausea into full force and it was all he could do to get out of his own way and puke over the side of whatever it was he lying on.

Sliding back down to his original prone position, he still felt incredibly ill, but he was able to think just a little clearer now that the urgency of vomiting was gone, even though his entire world was shifting and unstable. When the pounding of his own heartbeat finally stopped rushing in his ears, he became aware of a lapping sound, the slapping thud of waves against fiberglass. He must be on a boat, but why and where...

Groaning, he curled his bare arms and legs tightly against himself and tried to go back to sleep, willing it all to be a bad dream.

His throat was a fiery highway, his tongue a dead and bloated frog that could not reach his lips made of sandpaper. But with his blurry vision now registering shapes and dim light, Tyler forced his way back to consciousness. It was too much effort to move more than his eyeballs, but he could see the unfinished inside of a fiberglass hull and a tiny slit of a Plexiglas window.

After a while he forced himself to turn his head and was able to ascertain that he was indeed in the very small cabin of some sort of seafaring vessel. Barebones would barely describe the furnishings he could see – plastic–cushioned benches around three sides and a central tabletop covered in ragged black and white linoleum. At the far end of the interior were three steps leading to a closed hatchway; it could not have been more than twelve feet away but might as well have been twelve hundred.

With what seemed like an extreme amount of exertion, he managed to roll onto his back and throw one arm over his face. This was not a normal hangover, but that was all he was sure of. He could not remember a thing about how he had gotten here. He forced his scrambled mind to recall the events of the last few days. Had he been on a boat? The afternoon ride from Mustique to Bequia with Calvin came back to him. The bar with the band. Kip Kingsley's yacht in Lower Bay. Ingrid kissing a bald—headed man. Rudy and three black women in the sand.

Well, this sure as hell wasn't anybody's yacht. And he was pretty sure it wasn't even the same day.

The smell of his own vomit was suddenly overwhelming and made him want to hurl again. He had to get that hatch open and get out on deck. The sheer effort of moving was almost staggering as he crawled aft. When he pulled the handle there was a split second of terror that he might be locked in. But a moment later there was a creaking and then a sliding sound and his face was bathed in fresh sea air. He took only the briefest second to absorb that he was on a small speedboat before he flung himself down on the narrow deck and heaved over the side.

Unsteadily he fell back against the hatchway and at last surveyed his surroundings. What he discovered unnerved him more than his loss of memory. Despite the beauty of the glistening turquoise water and the warmth of the tropical sun, his outlook was decidedly bleak. He was adrift in the Caribbean Sea on a fifteen—foot motor boat – without a motor.

CHAPTER FOURTEEN

It wasn't until the third day that the tremors really began.

On the first day the misery had been equally divided between nausea, headache and thirst. Around sundown he found the half case of bottled water stowed in a compartment under the foremost bench and he knew he had a chance at survival. He used a soiled engine rag and half of a bottle of water to mop up the vomit on the cabin floor and then tossed it over the side, watching it sink to the depths of the darkening sea.

On the second day his suffering was split between hunger, boredom and the desire for an alcoholic beverage of any sort. He was tossed back and forth on the little boat as it bobbed in waves that seemed to be increasing in size as they drifted farther and farther from land. Sometimes he sat topside, clinging to the open hatchway, searching the shifting seascape for another boat. Occasionally he could see a white sail in the distance, like a shark fin on the horizon, but nothing came close enough for him to attract its attention. The Caribbean waters that had appeared so calm, inviting and well–traveled from shore now seemed desolate, deserted, and endless.

As soon as he felt well enough, Tyler searched his floating prison thoroughly, looking for clues to anything and everything. The boat was Spartan at best; the dust and mildew that covered most surfaces indicated it had been in disuse for some time. Although weather–beaten and colorless, it seemed to still be seaworthy and did not take on any water.

At first he could not figure why whoever had done this to him had not just dumped him overboard. But by the third morning, he realized that drifting aimlessly to a slow death by dehydration was a much crueler means of killing somebody than drowning.

He was sitting just inside the hatchway, staring aimlessly at the glare of the sunlight on the surface of the water when his left leg started to twitch uncontrollably. It was as though a nerve was pinched somewhere up by his hip, but there was nothing he could identify as the source of the problem. Perhaps it was merely from fear or anxiety, but soon his hands began to shake also and before he knew what was happening he was lying on his side, curled into a fetal position, sobbing and moaning from his own lack of restraint.

He'd never really had to admit to his alcoholism before; he'd spent the last few decades of his life always within close proximity to his next drink. But what had once seemed like a craving with the promise of sweet fulfillment just around the bend had now became a beckoning mirage, like the false hope of an oasis to a dying man crawling through the desert.

Time passed in a surreal way. He had moments, sometimes hours, of lucidity, but the hopelessness of his reality was no less a nightmare than the hallucinations that assaulted him each time he drifted out of consciousness. Golden beaches became quicksand that suffocated him and filled his lungs with cloying moist earth, gentle lapping waters on the shore became dark purple whirlpools of demonic chaos.

Images of old friends alternately tempted and tormented him. Sarah coming into the inn in Vermont with her cross–country skis on her shoulder, cheeks rosy from the icy winter air, the laughter on her lips suddenly twisting into the snarl of a mountain lion, fangs bared and ready to rip into his flesh. A topless Lucy with long fiery red hair, waving and smiling like a

159

mermaid from her perch on a rock at the end of Lower Bay and then the lower half of her body morphing into actual fish scales and tail as she was called to be rescued, her smile now a grimace of fright and helplessness, her hair snarled on an iron hook jutting out of the cliff behind her head, her breasts growing larger and more disproportionate by the second until their massiveness took over her entire being and she disappeared behind their immense swelling.

He cried so much he couldn't breathe and thought he might very well drown in his own tears. He couldn't understand how he could be crying all over his face, even on his forehead and ears. He opened his eyes to a thick enveloping blackness and realized it was night and he was lying with his head on the deck in an intense thunderstorm. The wind had picked up, the sea had become wild and the little boat was tossed about in the rain.

Retreating into the stifling cabin, he let himself be bashed mercilessly from side to side against the interior walls like a self–flagellating monk, until he howled with pain and passed into merciful unconsciousness.

When he next awoke, the sea was calm again and the sun was high. His head throbbed and his stomach ached with hunger. Fighting his way out of a dizzying haze, he opened another bottle of water and downed it thirstily before crawling weakly onto the deck.

Just another day in paradise. He collapsed against the railing and noticed his arm was bleeding. Still alive. Dipping his finger into the warm blood he wrote his name in a thin red script on the deck. A distant drone overhead grew louder and Tyler looked up to see a twin–engine prop plane flying high above him. If only there was some way to draw its attention. As it disappeared into the distance, he gazed morosely at his oozing cut. And finally a thought occurred to him...

It took him the rest of the daylight hours to finish the job. His plan would either save him or kill him – but that was how his life had always been, heads or tails, there was really nothing in between. He was lightheaded and exhausted by the time the sun sunk below the horizon; in his hallucinatory state he was sure he saw the elusive green flash of the sunset as the last rays dipped into the sea. But his task was accomplished.

Dried blood marked the scars on both of his arms and legs where he had ripped his flesh again and again with the rusty end of a nail that protruded from beneath the crudely constructed bunk. Countless times he had hauled himself above deck to the top of the cabin to squeeze his freshest wound onto blood–encrusted fingers and paint the oversized letters that signaled distress in any western culture. By the time he finished the last 'S' he was so aching and dehydrated he could only fling himself facedown below the message, his abused body an ironic underscore to the streaky red–brown S.O.S. now visible to any small aircraft that might fly overhead.

There was nothing more he could do now but drink water and wait.

Time lost all its meaning. Sometimes it was dark, sometimes light. At night the stars swirled dizzily overhead, a twinkling vortex that threatened to suck him away into the endless void of the universe, a fate which not be worse than his current situation. He fantasized about an alien spaceship landing, being gently lifted by one–eyed creatures with multiple arms who healed him instantly with the magic touch of a long electric finger. Like E.T. Phone home. He could not picture home anymore, he had lived so many places in his life. An image drifted through his mind of a hot little bungalow on a hillside in Grenada but it brought no sense of love or attachment. He did remember cool soft sheets and the comfort of a pillow and the secure sensation of being surrounded on all sides by mosquito netting.

The sun in the sky was more disorienting than the stars. In and out of consciousness now, he was never sure if it was going up or down, but its brightness hurt his eyes and made his parched throat feel even drier. The cuts on his arms and legs ached and oozed and in lucid moments he washed his wounds carefully with his now dwindling supply of bottled water and tried not to think about blood poisoning.

Much of the time he dreamed about food, favorites from his childhood that he hadn't eaten in years – luscious hunky slices of chocolate cake, cheeseburgers with lettuce and tomato, macaroni and cheese baked with a crispy crust, toast, butter, ice cream, orange juice…Sometimes he licked and sucked on his salty skin and pretended he was tasting and consuming a delicious meal.

But mostly he just slept and tried to remind himself to drink water. He rarely crawled to the edge of the deck to pee over the side anymore and he knew this was a bad indication of his dehydration level. He told himself he had lived a decent life, he had done the best he could and had never intentionally hurt anyone. He had a frequent hallucination now of Lucy and Tucker Brookstone playing on the beach in Lower Bay, it was a peaceful, comforting vision and he tried to keep it always handy in the front of his mind, to replace the dark fears that cast shadows over his perceptions.

His fitful naps eventually grew into longer and longer periods of sleep. He craved the escape that sleep brought, the escape from his damaged life. He was so tired. And hot. Sleeping forever seemed as if it was the only thing that he still knew how to do.

He was dreaming that he was stretched out on a cool and cushioned surface, everything around him light and white. Somebody was sponging his forehead with a damp cloth, and a cool breeze was blowing over him. He could feel himself rising to consciousness and didn't want to leave this dream, it was so pleasant and comfortable, so real.

"No, no, please, oh please," he moaned.

The sponging stopped suddenly and he knew it was over. He had to let go.

"Call de doctah," he heard a woman's deep voice say. "Him awake."

It took a few days before Tyler figured out that he was in the hospital on St. Vincent. As he slowly rehydrated back to life, he learned the details of his rescue from his night–time nurse, Delijah, a strapping woman with a throaty chuckle and soft dark skin that felt like heaven whenever it grazed over his own sunburned scales.

Apparently a small private aircraft bound for Mustique had spotted his little boat drifting about thirty miles offshore and a closer look through binoculars had revealed his bloody S.O.S. The coast guard had been radioed with the coordinates and two launches had been dispatched (Tyler was surprised to learn there was actually more than one coast guard boat available). His nearly lifeless body had been sped back to the little Bequia hospital where it was determined he needed more care than they could provide and he was immediately airlifted to St. Vincent.

His infected cuts were of almost more concern than his emaciated condition to the physician on–duty, who started him on an IV of antibiotics to reduce the chance of staph and blood poisoning, which evidently he had narrowly avoided.

On the third day he awoke from an afternoon nap to find Calvin sitting in the molded plastic chair next to his hospital bed. With characteristic enthusiasm, Calvin threw his arms around Tyler's neck and kissed him all over his face, uttering a stream of, what Tyler could only guess to be, patois prayers of joy and thanks.

"Meestah Mahckenzie, me nevah tink me see ya ugly mug again in me lifetime nah! We sure you gone wash up dead–dead on de rocks. Dis is one miracle of de church kine, yes, mon..."

Calvin beamed at him with tear–filled eyes. "So tell me, brudda, what happen to you dat day?" He lowered his voice. "Dem Apoplexica people do dis terrible ting to you?"

"I don't know," Tyler replied hesitantly. "I think probably. I think one of them slipped a mickey into a beer they sent over for me – put some kind of drug in it," Tyler explained upon seeing Calvin's blank look. "I remembering going into the water and then I must have passed out. Next thing I knew I was on a boat to nowhere." He shuddered involuntarily, trying not to remember his days at sea.

"You miss de whole Christmas you know, Boxing Day, everyt'ing. We try to have one good party but we all worrying about you."

Tyler still was not sure how long he had been gone. It had been a Sunday when he disappeared, he knew that much, but he had long ago lost track of actual dates.

"Justine she keep workin' at de Friendship Bay place, you know, painting for dem. She say she have something important to tell you, but she not trust me wid de informations."

Despite the close air of the hospital room, Tyler suddenly shivered. He had all but forgotten the mission he had left Justine on. Working every day in the same house as the bastards who had set him adrift and left him for dead. He had to get back to Bequia.

"Calvin, you need to get them to let me out of this place as soon as possible," he begged urgently.

"You not ready, mon. You too weaky–weak still. We can't risk it." Calvin crossed his arms defiantly and sat back, his stocky frame filling the plastic chair.

Tyler swore under his breath. "How soon to Old Year's Night?"

"Two days. But you can't go to De Reef party, mon. They will all be there – Kingsley and him band, Apoplexica men and women… what you thinkin'?"

"No, but you can be there. And I can be in Friendship Bay when they are not. I need to be out of here by then." Tyler struggled to an upright position. "Calvin, tell them to bring me some food. I'm ready to get strong. And we need to make a plan."

CHAPTER FIFTEEN

Barefoot in the sand and shrouded by the cover of a moonless sky, Tyler watched the lively scene inside De Reef. It was just past midnight, already New Year's Day really, and the party was just getting started. Revelers lined up at the bar for armloads of drinks, squeezed their way into the growing crowd on the dance floor, and got ready to party until dawn.

A plump woman in a tiny sequined mini dress squealed with carnal enjoyment as a tall dreadlocked man ground his body against her dazzling buttocks; a muscular fisherman, his unshaven face and upper chest glossy with sweat, gyrated alone with his arms above his head and a bottle of beer in each hand; a pair of vacationing European girls in skimpy neon bikini tops and rhinestone–studded denim shorts painfully bumped their sunburned shoulders and scraped their bare backs against the other partiers in the throng. Tyler could see Calvin inching his way toward this duo of ponytailed blondes, his testosterone level a more powerful navigation device than any electronic GPS system. In another venue, he would have appeared a suspicious character in his dark wraparound sunglasses and yellow baseball cap, but in Bequia on Old Year's Night he was just another quirky partygoer who had probably smoked just a few tokes too many before heading to De Reef.

On the stage, a ragged local reggae band was just finishing up its set and getting ready to dismantle their instrumental gear while the tech crew for Apoplexica set up drums and sound equipment for the main show of the night, which was rumored to start around two in the morning. Tyler scanned the crowd for the band members and then froze; just a few yards from where he was hidden in the shadows, Kip Kingsley, Eric Sands and their entourages were dining at a special table set out on the beach under a string of multicolored blinking lights.

He did a quick head count to make sure they were all there. Bald bass player, pierced drummer, wives, girlfriends, Brian the road manager.– Apoplexica, all present. He searched the other faces, trying to account for the members of Kingsley's band and was momentarily distracted by Jadene, more stunning than ever in a sleek yellow dress with a gravity–defying neckline that ended below her waist and that must have been stuck to her breasts with double–sided tape. Everyone was there, including Rudy who leaned against a post at the edge of the dance floor, sipping a rum and coke and keeping a silent vigil over the table – Tyler wondered who was guarding the yacht.

Too bad Ingrid was not around to give him the inside scoop tonight. When Tyler returned from the hospital, he discovered that Ingrid had gone home to Sweden for the Christmas holidays, abandoning her position as part of the "investigative" team when Tyler had mysteriously disappeared more than two weeks earlier. However, on that fateful afternoon, she had done her work well (as Tyler tried not to recall). Calvin had been anxious to report to Tyler what she had learned, but Justine had insisted he not say a word about it until Tyler was out of the hospital and back at the house on Bequia.

"Smugglers – de baddest kine," Calvin informed him when they were finally safely at the kitchen table again. "Not just de usual ganja. Dey running de coke from Columbia and de guns from Venezuela and probably more."

It was pretty much what Tyler had learned from his own experience on the yacht, but he still wanted to know how Ingrid had managed to learn this information.

"Dat woman she have her ways. She get people, especially de men, to trust her. Look at how she do you, mon."

As much as he hated to acknowledge the fact, he knew it was true. "Yeah, but I do her as much as she do me, mon," he admitted ruefully, trying not to associate their relationship with the nymphomaniac he had listened to on the sunset cruise to Friendship Bay. "So tell me how she found out and then I will tell you what I remember of that day."

Much as he wanted him to hurry the story along, Tyler had let Calvin enjoy spinning the tale of Ingrid undercover, before he filled in the details that he himself knew of that Sunday afternoon and evening when had been drugged and set adrift to die. And then, when Justine had finally arrived at the house, there was a replay of the emotional scene in the hospital the day before, with much hugging and tears and Caribbean cursing. Tyler savored the strength of her embrace and the softness of her skin as he buried his face in her shoulder. He felt her tears wash over him before she pushed him away and began shouting at him for making her so pathetic.

Finally, after wiping her eyes on a dish towel, she joined them at the table, and Tyler repeated his own account of the events, Justine shared what she had learned in her hours painting at the Friendship Bay house and then, together, they planned what to do next.

So here they were, less than twenty–four hours later, headed towards the end of the story. Tyler could admit that he was actually relieved at not having to deal with Ingrid's slippery two–sided personality or "succulent sluttiness" anymore and he was enjoying having her room to himself for the last few days. The inner emptiness he had been feeling since his detox on the boat was unnerving, yet strangely peaceful at times. It was painfully obvious now that he had only been in "lust" with Ingrid and he also questioned the root of his affection for Justine.

In reality there was only one true love of his life that he was mourning. He missed nothing as much as the sweet kiss of rum on his lips, the tingle of its distilled pureness on his tongue, the fiery burn of every delicious swallow. His heart ached for the constant companionship of Mount Gay with lime, or its always available cousin, an ice cold bottle of Carib. Watching the customers inside De Reef lovingly hold their drinks close was like being betrayed by a long–standing girlfriend, he wanted to know her comfort again, lose himself inside her warmth and numb the clarity of his existence.

He knew he would not go forever without drinking again, but for now it seemed a necessary discipline.

Suddenly his desire for alcohol was so strong, he realized had to get out of there and on to the next step of the evening's plan. With a tight throat and an iron heart, he turned his back on the bright lights of the celebration and moved off into the darkness of the beach.

Out on the road, he stopped to speak with a gangly boy lurking in the bush, and pressed a fifty cent coin into his hand. "Time has come – tell Calvin I am gone."

"Yes, mon." Like a conger eel, the youth slipped silently away.

Tyler walked swiftly through the village, against the tide of human traffic headed towards De Reef. Every few moments he would have to duck his head against the blinding illumination of the headlights from oncoming cars and taxis, hoping to avoid recognition. He made his way up the steeply winding hill, breathing heavily. He definitely did not have all his strength back yet. Pausing at a bend in the road, he took a break to gaze out at the bay where the lights on the sailboat masts created a twinkling constellation that was always in motion. Bequia had grown on him, and tonight he hoped to put the demons associated with it to rest.

At the top of the hill, a local woman approached him. She was wearing a loose shapeless dress and a dark bandana tied around her head and she carried a basket of tangerines on one arm. "I tink you need some of dis here fruit, mister mon," she said.

"And I tink you should walk with me down Friendship Bay way, sister, and talk about how much this fruit of yours will cost me." He fell in step with Justine, her brilliance and beauty well hidden in her shabby disguise.

"It almost already cost you your life. Me hope it na so expensive as dat tonight."

"Your friend the police officer know about this fruit you be selling this evening?"

"He do. Him waitin' for me call him." She patted the tangerines and with a quick flick of a finger indicated the cell phone concealed in the depths of the basket. "You see dem band playin' at De Reef fuh pahty?"

"Yes, mam. They settin' up right now." Despite the tense anticipation of the situation, Tyler was enjoying this playacting with Justine, and put his arm around her, saying the appropriate next words. "What you say, Miss Fruit Lady, you like me taste your juicy fruits tonight?"

"Woah, you foo foo tourist mon!" Her mirth was deep and throaty. "Me nah want your nasty man ting in me sweet lady parts. You keep dem ugly pants on unless me say you take dem off!" But she leaned into him in a flirtatious island girl manner as they passed another couple walking hand in hand along the side of the road.

"Woman, someday you gotta let this mortal man worship at your heavenly gates." He let his hand slip down to ride on the bounce of her well–rounded behind.

"Me like me a mon with more flesh on him – you too skin–and–bone fuh me, boy."

"What you say – me bone is fuh you?" They laughed together and Tyler gave her softness a squeeze before reluctantly letting her go. "Almost there," he murmured under his breath. "Got the key?"

"Of course, what you take me fuh?" As they walked beneath a streetlamp, she stopped and held out a tangerine to him. "Only one EC. Good for de Old Year's Night hangover."

A few yards away, a pair of young white men hiking up the hill looked eagerly at what she was offering. With a quick glance in their direction, Tyler put his mouth against her ear and said in a loud whisper, "I know something you have that would make me feel even better."

Against a background chorus of snickers, she gave him a merry slap. "Me boyfrien' bigguh den you puny bastard and he nah like what you sayin' to me."

If he had not been positioned on the uphill side of the road facing the bay, he would not have seen the two quick flashes of light; swift but evenly spaced. "The signal," he murmured, touching Justine's arm in a more serious fashion.

She froze and they both looked up at the cupola on the house across the road. Seconds later they saw the responding signal of a powerful torch, rapid yet deliberate.

"It's show time." Tyler shivered involuntarily. Justine pressed a pair of keys into his hand.

"You remember the alarm code?" she asked. He nodded. "Go. Now."

"Count to sixty and make that call," he said and disappeared hastily into the shadows. And although his racing heartbeat was loud in his ears, the impending satisfaction of justice and revenge propelled him forward.

There was no illumination around the door to the Sands mansion; no doubt it was kept purposely in darkness tonight. With trembling fingers, he inserted the keys into the deadbolt and the knob, and let himself inside. The foyer was dimly lit but the alarm keypad glowed green against the wall. He did not realize he had been holding his breath until he finally exhaled it as the code was accepted and the machine disarmed.

Slipping off his sandals, he moved soundless towards the cellar stairs and descended into the coolness below. On the last step, he stopped short. The door to the basement supply room was open, the padlock hanging loosely from the hasp. The eerie blue light of a fluorescent fixture spilled into the hall. Seconds later he could hear familiar voices arguing from within the space.

"Shit. Look at all this fuckin' cash. Don't suppose they'd miss a few quid off the top, do you?"

"Don't be an idiot and fuck this thing up. Whose asses do you think it'll be if it's not all there when they count it later? Now take a couple of these bags and haul them up to the back door."

Lenny and Gustav, the two from the yacht.

Tyler had to get out of sight. Now. As stealthily as possible, he glided across the concrete floor in the direction of the laundry room door which was open just a crack. He had barely slid inside when the two came crashing out into the hallway, still yelling at each other.

"Christ, who knew money could be so heavy. Why couldn't they just arrange an electronic deposit into a Swiss bank or something."

"You need to take up fuckin' weightlifting or something. Lifting beers don't seem to be givin' you the muscle you need for this gig."

"You should talk. I don't see you taking the steps two at a freakin' time."

. Tyler flattened himself into a narrow space between the washing machine and the wall. Breathing heavily, he tried to figure out what part of the plan he had stumbled into. The pay–off, apparently, but how was it going to work.

As their voices faded off momentarily, he peered out of the laundry room. The open door with the hinged hasp was just a few feet away; the padlock itself hung freely on the steel hook on the other side of the door frame. A crazy idea flashed through his mind; before he let himself reconsider he sprang out into the hallway and in a few giant strides he had reached the gleaming lock, carefully removed it, and darted back to his hiding place.

Seconds later Lenny and Gustav came clambering down the stairs.

"We could take just one of these bags, jack a motorboat and be halfway to Barbados before they found us, you know."

"Like you know which direction Barbados is."

"I got a GPS in my phone."

"Which don't even work in the Caribbean."

Before Tyler could make his move, they were headed back upstairs again, grunting under another load. He didn't know how many more opportunities he was going to get, he would have to take his chances as soon as they returned.

Even in the dank air, he felt a trickle of sweat run down the side of his face. His palms were so damp he feared losing his grip on the lock. A pair of mosquitos buzzed around his ankles but he didn't dare to swat them.

"One more trip. Come on, they'll be here any minute."

"Cool your heels, we've got time."

Tyler heard the click–click of a lighter and then the harsh smell of ganja smoke tickled his nostrils.

"Want a hit?"

"Not right now, asshole. Get in here and grab those last two in the corner."

Sparks were going off inside his brain – there was no time for thinking anymore. Tyler sprang out from behind the wall and, in one swift motion, pushed the door shut, hitched the padlock through the hasp, and snapped it securely into place.

And then, sliding to the floor, he closed his eyes as the frantic pounding from the other side of the door resounded dully throughout the house.

CHAPTER SIXTEEN

Dawn was barely breaking as Tyler stumbled onto the sand of Lower Bay Beach. Despite, or perhaps as a result of, the arrest of the band members of Apoplexica, the party at De Reef was still going on, although the music that throbbed from the oversized speakers was no longer live. Drunken and disheveled revelers staggered in the opposite direction now, headed home or back to their hotels. Angry shouts and arguments could be heard spontaneously erupting from the vicinity of the bar, the excitement and unexpected outcome of the night being more than many of the inebriated carousers could handle.

Exhausted yet exhilarated, he sat heavily on the wide root of an overhanging manchioneal tree, watching the sky grow lighter and contemplating the events of the last several hours. It had been a wild night on the island. But Tyler knew that soon enough the dust would settle and the story of the Old Year's Night bust would become just one more tale spun out on hot Sunday afternoons over rum punch and fried fish at De Reef.

He did not know how long he had sat against the door to the supply room, minutes, hours, but at some point he realized that he had to get out of the house before the police arrived. Dashing back up the stairs, he was on the other side of the front door before he realized he had left his sandals in the corner of the laundry room. A small price to pay, and he certainly wasn't going to be the only person on the island that night who would lose their shoes in the heat of the moment.

"What happen?" Justine asked anxiously as he suddenly materialized at her side.

"Change of plans." He had barely gasped the words when they heard a car winding its way up the hill from the bay, its engine roaring with the downshifting of gears. At the same time, the sound of several vehicles coming down the road reached their ears. Seconds later, a black truck veered into the steep driveway of the mansion just as three Land Rovers came around the corner and screeched to a stop, one of them neatly blocking the end of the drive and the escape route of whoever had just pulled in. Twelve policemen leaped out of the jeeps. Brandishing their machine guns with overenthusiastic authority and purpose, they proceeded to surround the house.

Tyler drew Justine farther back into the protective shadows of a mango tree behind them. They both froze as a buzzing vibration began emanating from the basket of tangerines. "The phone," she whispered. "It Calvin." Her hand fumbled in the fruit and then quickly moved to her ear. "What?" she murmured. "Okay. De police dem here." Flicking the phone shut, she looked up at Tyler. Even in the darkness, he could see her eyes, fearful and shining. "It done."

He removed the phone from her trembling fingers and slipped it deep into the pocket of his shorts just as spotlights illuminated the house and a megaphone boomed an unintelligible warning.

Justine touched his arm. "Look." She nodded down towards the bay where an unnatural brightness was lighting up the water and the sky. "Must be the coast guard also."

Tyler felt the warmth of vindication. After all these years, the wheels of justice he were turning at last.

It seemed like hours before they saw Lenny and Gustav marched down the driveway in handcuffs and shoved unceremoniously into the back of a Land Rover. They were followed by a squat, swarthy man wearing a black bandana tied around his head and sporting an open fatigue vest that displayed his robust arms and bare chest.

"A pirate if I ever saw one," Tyler commented, feeling a certain sense of satisfaction. The excitement had drawn a neighborhood crowd and Tyler and Justine had abandoned their hiding place to join the enthralled bystanders.

"Investigator, I believe our work is done here." Justine's imitation of a British accent made him smile, releasing the tense muscles of his face to relax.

"Then let's see if we can get over to Lower Bay in time for the next act." Arm in arm, they headed back over the hill.

But as they descended the steep roadway down the other side of the island, they were forced to quickly jump into the gutter as the three Land Rovers whizzed past, taking the hairpin turns at precarious speed. By the time Tyler and Justine approached De Reef, they could not even get close. Barricades spanned the width of the street and throngs of people were shouting angrily and shoving each other to get a better look at the action.

"What's going on?" Tyler asked the nearest onlooker, feigning innocence.

"Dem police taking de band away! It not right, mon! Dem wreckin' de party mood!" He punctuated his tirade by smashing an empty Hairoun bottle on the edge of the road.

Although the soles of his feet were weathered and toughened by his many years in the islands, Tyler winced at the prospect of continuing on barefoot through the maddening crowd. "There's no way we can get to the house," he shouted to Justine. "Let's try the beach."

"I can do it," she assured him. "I'll cut up by Sylvester's and take the footpath. You go down by the sea. I will catch up with you." And then, hoisting the basket onto her head, she shouldered her way into the tightly packed bodies with the ease of a cobra slithering through the jungle underbrush.

Tyler gingerly began to inch towards the beach but he was moving against the human tide that was desperate to get closer to the spectacle taking place at De Reef. The stench of breath soured by cheap beer and stale ganja smoke was overpowering and added to his growing sense of claustrophobia. He reminded himself that he was safe here, just a face in the crowd, and yet he felt as though he were suffocating in the escalating agitation of the moment and the crush of sweating bodies.

When he finally broke free, he staggered unsteadily into the rough grass and prickly underbrush that separated the beach from the road. Mindless of the hazards beneath his feet and the branches scratching his arms and legs, he stumbled through the darkness, tripping into the dampness of the sand and landing hard on his side.

The sound of his own inhaling and exhaling filled his head for a moment, blocking out the rest of the night. Pulling himself to a sitting position, he was suddenly aware of that the commotion had extended out into the harbor. Sirens blared and high beams flashed, lighting up a large yacht that Tyler recognized as Kingsley's.

Calvin's sting was happening. It had not been part of Tyler's original plan, but Calvin had been insistent. "That bloodclot need to be taught a lesson and we not want him comin' back here to dis island any time soon." Tyler did not ask where or how or what Calvin was contriving, but he knew it involved planting a large of amount of illegal substances on Kip's boat.

"I am not down with this, man," Tyler warned him. "If you get caught—"

"No worries," Calvin promised. "I want to see de motherfucka fry."

What the fuck, what did it matter in the end, he thought pessimistically. Would they all go to jail, the Apoplexica gang and their Boneyard friends? Someone would be left on the outside, only the main players would be implicated and charged, and it was likely that Tyler would still always be watching his back, still shivering inside when he heard their songs played in a bar, still worrying that someday he would get into a car and a bomb would explode.

With a cry of rage, he leaped to his feet and shook himself violently, trying to rid his mind of the thoughts and images that threatened to overtake his spirit again. It was done, it was over. He could hear a change in the noise of the crowd up on the road now, as the horns of the police vehicles began honking to announce that they were coming through.

The soothing sound of the surf licking at the shore beckoned him, luring him into its soft, wet caress, lapping at his ankles and his knees, drenching the thin fabric of his shorts, seducing him with its moist touch, until finally he dove beneath the surface, succumbing to its comforting embrace.

Eventually he rose from the depths, dripping like a lagoon creature and reeling like a baptized revivalist. Refreshed and reinvigorated, he walked briskly in the direction of De Reef, ready for the rest of the evening's aftermath.

He got there in time to see the smirk on Kip Kingsley's face disappear as he was led away from the bar, hauled through a crowd that was now howling and berserk with too much excitement,. his arms secured behind him by two oversized officers,

"Dey run out of handcuffs," said a voice next to his ear.

Calvin's beaming grin belied the exhaustion in his bloodshot eyes as he embraced Tyler in a crushing bear hug. Only the dampness of his yellow nylon shorts indicated he had been any place other than partying his brains out all night.

"Thought you might need some of this by now." Justine's voice broke through Tyler's contemplations of the events of the last few hours. He gratefully accepted the hot cup of coffee she held out to him.

He looked over at her as she seated herself on the sand beside him and sipped from her own mug. She had changed out of her fruit lady clothes and now wore a loose white gauze shirt over snug, knee–length denim shorts. It was not her usual flamboyantly artistic, well–guarded style, in fact, it was as casual as he had ever seen her in public. She dug the heels of her wide brown feet into the sand and gazed at him with eyes as dark as the steaming liquid in her cup.

"So, Mr. Mackenzie."

"So, Miss Justine."

"Well done."

"Couldn't have done it withoutcha." He moved his foot across the sand to touch hers, in a tentative but familiar gesture.

"Guess it be time for you to think about leaving dis island."

Their eyes locked briefly before he shifted his gaze out to the horizon. Daylight was coming on fast now, infusing the sky with the ubiquitous coral pink of dawn.

"Well, don't think you are going to get rid of me so fast. I haven't really finished the task I was hired to come here and do. The job I was hired for."

"Finding Lucy."

"Finding Lucy's son."

A silence fell between them, deep and complex, as they both considered in their own way, what had to happen next. In the fray of the last few days, Tyler had indeed lost sight of his original objective for being on Bequia. He still didn't know where in the world Tucker Brookstone was.

"Can you unlock the school for me in a while? I need to use the computer."

"Yes, but first, where is de mobile phone you take from me? I need to return it to de friend who loan it."

"The...oh, no." Tyler patted the pockets of his shorts and then sheepishly withdrew the object in question. "Uh..." he flipped it open and pressed a few buttons. "I think I owe your friend a new phone."

Tyler realized he had not been online in weeks. He'd been awake for more than twenty–four hours, but despite his exhaustion, he was compelled to renew his efforts to keep his promise to Lucy's sister. If nothing else, he owed her a call. And he was pretty sure Ingrid had Skype installed on her system so she could stay in touch with her friends and family back in Sweden.

He nearly fell asleep listening to the slow whir of the computer as it booted up and came to life. Sure enough, there was the Skype icon in the taskbar. He clicked on it, sleepily watching it load up with Ingrid's contacts. A name caught his eye and suddenly he was wide awake, scrolling back through the names to make sure he had seen correctly. There it was. Ruby Mackenzie. Lucy's alias. He clicked on the name and found he had the option to "show messages from Yesterday, 7 days, 30 days, 3 months, 6 months, 1 year."

He worked his way back, checking each of the options. Nothing on Yesterday or 7 Days, but on 30 Days he hit the mother lode. His eyes widened as he read the messageson the screen. "Call to Ruby Mackenzie, duration 31:52. Call from Ruby Mackenzie, duration 15:37." When had he first arrived on Bequia...it had to have been just about a month now. So these calls had happened since then. He did not fully understand what he was seeing but the implications roared through his head like a freight train.

He had to check his email messages, get the number for Amelia, give her a call. He opened Internet

Explorer and found himself again riveted to the molded plastic lawn chair he was sitting on. Ingrid had forgotten to sign out of her email account. He watched as the new emails came in, one after another, and when they finally stopped loading, he scrolled down the screen and paged back, again and again, until once again the name he was searching for showed up on the screen. On November 30th, Ruby Mackenzie had sent an email, subject line: Arrived Safely.

"All is well," the message read. "S has made us feel right at home. T is going to school in the village, and I finally feel we are safe. Can't get used to the weather; I never take off my sweater. Any sign of you know who yet? I'll Skype you soon."

What the fuck was this... If he thought he had been tense when breaking into the house in Friendship Bay, well he was wrong; a whole new level of tension gripped his soul.

He quickly flipped to a new window and logged into his own email account. He quickly scanned his messages, but between the holiday greetings from his family and the promotional junk, he could find no new emails from Amelia. Then he scrolled back a few pages until he located the original email she had sent him. Switching to Skype, he typed in the UK phone number.

"We're sorry but the number you are calling is not in service. Please make sure you are dialing the correct number and try your call again."

What the fuck, he said again. His rusty web skills were coming back to him. He did a search on a phone number for Amelia Rigby in the London area and within seconds he was keying the number into the Skype phone pad.

"Rigby residence." The voice that answered was hoarse and unfamiliar.

"Tyler Mackenzie here. Is Amelia there?"

"Amelia? No, of course she's not." A harsh cackle was followed by a bout of coughing.

"Oh, I'm sorry. Has her, uh, time come?" He'd forgotten about the advanced pregnancy.

"Her time? Whatever are you referring to? What are you selling?"

"Selling – sorry, no, I'm not a salesman. She hired me to find her nephew. Can I leave her a message?"

Another croaking chuckle. "You can, but I doubt that she'll receive it. She hasn't been back from Dubai for the last 3 years."

"Dubai? But she called me last month..."

"Not from here, she didn't. They haven't been back since Easter. If she rang you, it was from the UAE."

"Really." Tyler was beginning to doubt his own sanity. "Well, maybe she did. Would have that number?"

He could not find a pen, so instead he opened a new email and keyed the string of country codes, area codes and exchange numbers directly into the computer. "Thanks a lot. You've been really helpful. So do you know, is the baby due any day?"

"Baby? Are we talking about the same Amanda Rigby?"

Tyler hit the "End" button without replying. The raucous laughter told him all he needed to know.

As did the stony silence on the other end of the line when he identified himself to the unfamiliar voice that belonged to Amanda Rigby. "Have we met?"

"You hired me to find your nephew, Tucker, last month. After your sister, Lucy ..." his voice trailed off. There was no point in finishing the sentence. He knew what was coming next.

In spite of the early hour and the coolness of the darkened classroom, Tyler felt flushed and overheated. He spent a long 15 seconds considering his options before he chose Ruby Mackenzie out of Ingrid's list of Skype contacts.

He listened as the phone rang and rang again, not wanting to hang up on the possibilities that dangled just out of reach in the endless configurations of his imagination. He realized he had not considered the time – the clock in the corner of the computer said 8am – but then again, he had no idea where in the world he was calling.

And then suddenly the ringing stopped and the screen froze before flickering jerkily to life. A human form appeared in broken digital images – wide eyes staring back at him across the ethers – and then the image darted away, shouting as it ran, leaving Tyler with the view of an empty plaid couch against a wood–paneled wall.

"Mom! Auntie Ingrid is calling you! Mom!"

The picture froze again, suspended in the netherworld of long– distance cyber chat. There was nothing unusual about a slow internet speed or a bad connection on Bequia, but in these imminent circumstances, it was more than frustrating. Tyler pounded on the "Enter" key in exasperation, at the petrified freeze–frame of a living room that seemed familiar in a strange way, like a recurring dream that he knew the ending of before it even began...

The plastic chair flipped back over backwards as Tyler leaped to his feet, gaping in disbelief at what he was seeing. "Call Ended," flashed across the screen as the connection was lost. But it no longer mattered. All the pieces of the puzzle had finally fallen into place.

CHAPTER SEVENTEEN

When Justine found him, the bottle of rum was already half empty. He was sitting on the hard tiles of the bedroom floor, his head resting on the edge of the mattress, half–closed eyes staring sightlessly at the closet door in front of him.

"What the hell! What is wrong with you, you crazy mother..." Her swearing ascended into a crescendo of Caribbean patois as she attempted to wrest the liquor away from him. He tightened his grasp and with an angry squaring of his jaw, took another defiant swig.

With a cry of rage, Justine smacked him soundly across the side of his head, causing him to slide unsteadily to the floor, and stunning him just enough that she could quickly grab the bottle out of his tremulous fingers. He tried vainly to reach for it, but in his recently half–starved state he was no match for her stalwart strength. She pushed him down easily, holding him fast by his bony shoulders, using the weight of her solid body to restrain him.

Tyler struggled half–heartedly to free himself and then with a sigh, closed his eyes and went limp. "Why?" she whispered harshly. "Why now?"

"Why yourself," he mumbled and then his eyes flickered open and met hers in unforgiving accusation. "Why did you all lie to me?"

She squinted at him. "What are you talking about, Tyler? I have never lied to you."

"Oh, no?" He attempted to shake her loose, but she had him firmly pinned. "We all know Ingrid is a two–faced bitch, but you? And Calvin? I trusted you with everything..." He could feel his vision starting to blur with tears and he turned his face away. "I love you guys like family. And you've all been playing me, like some stupid game."

Justine had an inscrutable look on her face as she released her hold on him. She rose slowly to her feet and then helped Tyler to a standing position, but he felt too heavy to remain upright and sank down immediately onto the bed. In a swift and sudden motion, Justine picked up the open bottle of rum and heaved it out the open bedroom window.

The sound of glass shattering on the rocks below cut through the fog in Tyler's brain, bringing momentary clarity. "How long have you all known where she is?"

Justine still did not appear to comprehend what he was talking about.

"Lucy. 'Ruby.'" He added the alias in a mocking tone. "I know now that Ingrid has been in touch with her the whole time I've been here."

She perched on the end of the bed, staring at him and still saying nothing.

"Don't tell me you didn't know. The whole thing was a set–up to get me here. In fact, Lucy's sister, Amelia, who supposedly was paying me to find her nephew, was extremely upset and confused when I told her she had hired me and been footing my bills on Bequia."

Justine opened her mouth to speak and then closed it again. Tyler had never seen her speechless before and it emboldened him to continue.

"And freakin' Calvin. Acting so angry and righteous and...and...shocked. He should go to Hollywood; he might win an Oscar." But even as he spoke his thoughts aloud, Tyler began to question the logic of his rationale. "So tell me how it went – this was just some kind of trap to get me here for...for what?"

Justine seemed fixated on some vague spot on the wall behind him; she could not meet the fury of his contemptuous gaze.

"It not what you are thinking, you know," she replied finally. "We never even know her real name is Lucy. We only know her as Ruby. All of this is true – she tell us she is running from a man who abuse her. We never know it is the famous Kip Kingsley who she is hiding from."

Tyler fought his instinct to just lie down and not listen. He was starting to feel nauseous and dizzy from the effect of so much alcohol in his purified system and on an empty stomach as well. He leaned back on the pillows and crossed his arms. "Yeah, I've heard all this bullshit before. Why should I believe it now?"

"I would swear in church that not Calvin or I knew any different. It was Ingrid she was mostly close with. I didn't even move in to this house until she left Bequia."

He frowned, knowing this was true. "But you all helped her leave the island and lied to me about it."

"When you first came, we thought you were the rotten husband looking for her. You even had the same last name! We did what any real friends would do – we protected her." She reached for his hand and forced him to look at her honest expression. "Everything that has happened since, helping you, working with you, that has been real."

"But what the hell..." Tyler's head was spinning from more than just liquor now. "How did I end up here in the first place? Who called me, who set me up?"

She shook her head. "We were not expecting you. At least I wasn't. But it doesn't seem accidental, that you would somehow be facing the very people you ran away from half a decade ago."

"Okay, but Ingrid has been in touch with her since I've been here and she never told me. Here I am, struggling to figure out where Lucy and Tucker are and she has been in contact with them all along?" His voice rose accusingly. "I call that plain old deception."

"And how do you know this?"

"Because – because I saw it in her computer." Tyler told her about finding Ruby's name in Ingrid's Skype contacts and reading the emails between the two of them. It was true – in all the communication, she was still identified as Ruby. It was entirely possible that Ingrid had not known Ruby's true identity.

"So, it sounds to me that you being called to Bequia is the work of just one person. Someone who knows you really well and knew how you would respond."

He was silent for a few moments, contemplating the truth of this possibility. Actually there were two women in the world who knew him well enough to plan a scheme such as this one, who could appreciate the depths to which his existence had sunk in Grenada, having both known the overachieving pinnacles of his life before. Who would know which buttons to push if there was any hope of getting him out of the hole he had dug for himself.

Who would care whether or not he ever found little Tucker Brookstone.

"I know where she is," he croaked hoarsely. And then he leaned over the windowsill and puked his guts out into the bushes below.

Two days later he was back in Grenada, quietly picking up the pieces of what had once been his reality. But without the comfort of rum, none of it felt very satisfying and he knew he was just putting off the inevitable. Still, he needed the money to move on, although at Grenadian wages, it was going to take more than a few months to earn the cost of the airline ticket required to get off the island.

Seymour had given him his old job back, cooking at the Papaya Tree, and the days fell into their old empty sameness. It took superhuman effort to not slide back into his drinking habits but he knew that if wanted to get off the island, it was necessary to let his old friend alcohol go, at least for now.

After his time on Bequia, he had to tell Silvalyn it was over between them. His heart ached from his unrequited passion and bittersweet parting with Justine. Silvalyn did not let go easily – for several nights she pounded on his door, begging him to take her back. But now that he was no longer constantly numb with rum, he couldn't go back to the place he had been with her. At times he lay awake for hours, inside his mosquito–net, confused by his chaotic longings, yet aching for physical comfort and consolation.

A few months after his return, Justine showed up unexpectedly for a weekend. He came out of the kitchen after his evening shift to find her sitting at the bar drinking a ginger beer, looking beautifully regal and exquisitely out of place. Tyler felt his face break into a beaming grin for the first time in weeks.

"Well, hello, missy." He untied his apron and tossed it onto a chair. "Come here often?"

"Just checkin' up on you, Mr. Mackenzie." She tried to keep herself from smiling. "You been keeping yourself out of trouble?"

"I was until just now." Tentatively he reached over and stroked the soft, sensitive skin on the underside of her arm. "So – were you planning on staying at my place?"

"Boy, you be tinkin' I come all de way here from Bequia just to be stayin' in some hotel?" She somehow managed a look that was both bold and coy at the same time.

Gently he put his thumb under her chin. "You sure about this?"

"It be your job to make me so."

Forty–eight hours later she was gone, but for days afterwards Tyler glowed with an inner sense of warmth and fulfillment. It had been a long time since he had felt as close to anyone as Justine, and even though he knew that he would probably never see her again, their intimacy had made him feel complete.

It had come as no surprise to Tyler that, despite her commanding poise and presence, Justine had been shy and inexperienced when it came to sex. It had been a joy to spend hours in bed with her, first making her feel comfortable, then excited, and finally satisfied. He savored every moment and variation – skin on skin, lips on lips, lips on skin, skin on lips...

"Don't leave me," he begged her on the second morning as he wrapped himself around her from behind and buried his face into the sweetness of her neck, running his hands over the now familiar softness of her belly to rest on the tender fullness of her breasts.

The sigh that escaped her spanned both pleasure and sadness. "You'll always have me," she whispered. "But you know where you need to be heading now and I am not part of that story."

"You could be. Come with me."

"Don't be foo–foo. That cold mountain place is not for me," she scoffed.

"I'll keep you warm."

"There not enough flesh on your skinny bones to warm the likes of me."

"Oh, no? I thought I got the likes of you pretty hot in the last few days." He ran his tongue around the edge of her ear. "Why did you come here?" he asked.

"Why do you think?"

"Just say the words. So I can hear them." He rolled her onto her back and sat up so he could look down on her beautiful face.

She closed her eyes. "I wanted to be with you. Like this."

He felt flushed and alive. "Like this?" He leaned over her and kissed her dark nipples before straddling her waist. "Like this? Or like this? Or do you mean like this..."

Tyler borrowed Seymour's truck to drive Justine to the airport. Although neither spoke during the ride, the weight of their impending separation hung heavily in the space between them.

"Well, give my regards to everybody in Lower Bay," he said as pulled up to the curb in front of Departures. When she didn't reply, he looked over at her questioningly. "Or does nobody know where you actually went for the weekend?"

He didn't think he had ever seen her blush before. "You know how it is with me. What I do with my life is my business."

He grinned ruefully. "I do know."

She reached for his hand and he grasped it tightly. "Promise me one thing, Mr. Mackenzie."

"I will promise you anything."

"That you buy yourself some new clothes before you go north, boy! Your pants so raggedy you look like a beggar."

It was mid–April by the time Tyler landed in Burlington. If spring was in the air, no one had told northern Vermont. Dirty piles of plowed snow were still evident at the ends of the small runway and the air had a nip to it he had not felt in nearly six years. He was glad now that, when he dragged his suitcase out from under the bed, he had discovered the fleece jacket he had been wearing when he arrived in Grenada all those seasons ago. His running shoes had not fared as well over time, stiffening and cracking, but he had no other choice –flip–flops were not an option.

At the car rental counter, he also realized that his license and credit cards had also not endured his tenure in the Caribbean. He wasn't going far with those expiration dates. And there were definitely no buses traveling to the small rural towns of the Northeast Kingdom.

He couldn't remember the last time he had hitchhiked anywhere. After stepping through the automatic sliding doors and feeling the cold wind in his hair, he returned to the airport gift shop where he bought a pair of heavy woolen gloves and a knitted cap that bore the legend, "Ski Stowe."

One of his fellow passengers on the small prop plane from LaGuardia took pity on him and picked him up just outside the airport. Before long, he had made it as far as Montpelier, but he was not quite as lucky catching a ride from there. As he stood on the side of the road, the long journey began to catch up with him – he'd spent a day flying from Grenada to Miami to Washington, DC, where he'd had to spend the night in the airport before flying on to Burlington in the morning. His blood seemed to have thinned during his island years and the cool weather whipped through his bones. When finally a van of dreadlocked white boys stopped to pick him up, he felt immeasurably grateful and fell asleep almost instantly, lulled by the overheated air heavy with ganja smoke.

"Yo, dude. We're in Jordan Center. Isn't this where you're getting out?"

Tyler jerked awake and looked around disoriented. He'd been dreaming he was back at Grand Anse Beach but here he was in the gray midday light of northern Vermont.

"West Jordan," he mumbled, trying to get his bearings in the once familiar surroundings.

"That's the way to West Jordan over there. It's about five miles. You want a hit for the road?" Blond dreadlocks guy was holding out a joint to him.

"That's okay. Thanks for the ride, mon." He staggered out onto the asphalt and looked around. He knew where he was – he had traveled this road hundreds of times – but it hardly felt like home. He could call the inn now and someone would come get him, but he didn't want to do it that way. He wanted to get back on his own.

Shouldering his tattered daypack and dragging his suitcase behind him in the gravel, he headed for the West Jordan road and the final leg of his journey. Traffic was light this time of day and it took nearly an hour before a pickup truck finally slowed down to offer him a ride. The wizened driver looked at him quizzically as he shifted into gear and moved back out onto the highway.

"You remind me of someone. Don't I know you?"

Tyler gave a short snort of a laugh. "You might. I used to live around here. At the West Jordan Inn, with Sarah Scupper."

"Damn, of course, I remember you. The journalist guy from New York, right? You almost burned up in that old hotel about ten years ago, didn't you?"

Tyler laughed for real this time and felt his body relaxing inside its fleece–covered exterior. He'd forgotten how similar small town life was to being on an island. "Yes, that was me, wasn't it.? And you are..."

"Beau. Beau Boudreau, a regular at the WJ bar. That where you're headed?"

"Yes. Yes, I am. Thank you, Beau. How are things in West Jordan? Haven't been back in a long time."

"Ay–yuh – things are little different there now at the inn, what with all those kids running around all the time. And old man Sawyer sold his farm to a developer who's building condos. And they shut down the gas pumps at the village store. Post office is only open until 11 on Saturdays. That's about all I can think of."

But Tyler hadn't heard anything after the comment about the "kids" at the inn. He realized he had been in the Caribbean for more than five years and in London for another two – enough time for anything to happen – and he had no idea what he was walking into. When he disappeared to England with Lucy, he had bitterly left his former soulmate Sarah, to run the West Jordan Inn, with her new boyfriend and his adopted African baby. Since then, Tyler'd had little to no contact with Sarah. Of course, he'd had no contact with anybody really. And if it wasn't for the turn of events in the last few months, he would not be on his way here now.

"What's your name again?" the old man was asking him.

"Tyler. Tyler Mackenzie."

"And how long since you been here?"

"Seven years?"

"Well, Tyler, let me be the first to welcome you home."

By the time Beau drove his truck into the parking lot of the West Jordan Inn, Happy Hour had already started and he was ready for a drink. "Can I buy you one?" he offered, but Tyler declined and, avoiding the bar, headed around to the long porch at the front of the building. As he set his foot on the well–worn steps, the door banged open and a tall man with a long dark ponytail appeared, carrying a toddler in his arms and yelling over his shoulder. "Come on, Myles, get your jacket. Kashi is waiting for us at the dance studio."

A small boy darted out from behind him and skidded to a stop when he saw Tyler standing there in his path. "Dad?" he said uncertainly, looking back at his father.

"Hey, what can I do for you – sorry, we're kind of in a hurry here."

"Hunter. It's me, Tyler."

"Say what?! Tyler! Wow, this is so freakin' cool! How you doin', man?" Somehow Hunter managed to give Tyler a powerful hug while still holding on to the child. "What are you doing here? Shit, we gotta go pick Kashi up from dance class but we'll be back soon. Sarah's working the bar, go on in. She'd love to see you. You gonna be able to spend the night, I hope? Myles, this way, buddy, to the car!"

Hunter had not changed much in seven years —even then he had been good with kids, as Tyler ruefully remembered. As he let himself into the front office, he caught a glimpse of a Subaru station wagon tearing ass out onto the road, the bass line of the sound system trailing behind it.

And then he closed his eyes as the familiar smell of the inn overcame his senses – a mixture of musty pine flooring, spicy chili, wood smoke, down jackets and wool blankets with overtones of freshly brewed coffee and the faint undernote of stale beer. He leaned back against the doorframe, inhaling the familiarity of it all, the safety of its refuge making him feel insecure and unsure.

"Hunter, don't forget the milk— ohh, sorry. Can I help you?"

And there she was – it was over before he had any more time to anticipate it. Her freckles had faded a bit and her halo of curly red hair was shorter than he remembered it and the color was not quite the same, and her British accent seemed as out of place in Vermont as it always had. "I'm terribly sorry," she was saying now," but we don't have any rooms here if that's what you're looking for, we're just a bar and restaurant."

He cleared his throat. "Actually that's not what I'm looking for."

"Holy bloody shit." And before he had time to blink, Lucy's arms were around his neck and she was shrieking with delight. "I can't freakin' believe it! You did it – you actually found us."

Tyler was too exhausted and overcome with emotion to say anything but it didn't seem to matter. Lucy seemed to be able to do the talking for both of them. "Look at you – you are so thin and tan and what's up with this beard! How long did it take you, you must be so tired. Come inside and let's get you something to eat. Do you want a beer?"

He shook his head but she was already leading him towards the bar. "No, Lucy, no. I'm not drinking these days."

Her hand flew to her mouth as she apologized profusely. "Of course, what was I thinking –"

"Don't." He realized he could barely make conversation. "Let's just go upstairs and talk. I have a lot of...questions."

Without another word, she took him by the arm and steered him towards the narrow wooden staircase that led to the living quarters upstairs.

The first difference he noticed was the toys – they were everywhere. Legos and Barbies were scattered along the hallway. Crayons and paper were lined up against the walls between blocks and balls and toy trucks. What had once been the inn's old–fashioned guest rooms were now painted bright – lime, purple, magenta – and strewn with a jumble of printed quilts and colorful articles of clothing.

Lucy stopped in the kitchen to fill a glass with water and handed it to him before moving on. Tyler noted that although the counters were cluttered with appliances and other culinary accoutrements, the dishes were washed and drying in the drainer and a large pot of something was simmering on the stove. One end of the long dining room table was piled high with backpacks and schoolbooks; the other end was hosting an elaborate science project created of clay and sticks.

Amazingly, the living room was orderly and clean.

Lucy sat down abruptly on the couch and suddenly there was an awkwardness between them; Tyler settled in at the opposite end, feeling flushed and overheated. He realized that he was still wearing his jacket and cap, unused to the rituals of wearing outerwear and removing it indoors. He undressed slowly, putting off the moment of confrontation for a few more seconds.

"So. Somehow I get the feeling you don't want to make small talk then." Lucy attempted a grin. "I just want to say again how glad I am to see you in the flesh."

"Why don't we just start at the beginning."

"You mean back in London? When I left or you left?"

Tyler swallowed some water. "No, let's come back to that. Let's start with where you faked your own death and had someone impersonate your sister to call me about it and convince me in my grief to go to Bequia. Did I react the way you wanted me to?"

Lucy sighed and looked at her lap. "I'm sorry. I knew I had to do something extreme."

"Because...?"

"Because clearly you were drowning in your own depression. Sarah had completely lost track of you, no one in your family had seen you in years, they rarely heard from you and the most they could tell me was that you were on the island of Grenada and had completely given up anything to do with your career. I still have a few friends in the business and had them do a little investigating on you and after what they told me—"

"You had people following me?" He laughed bitterly. "Wait — before we even go there, answer me this — what are you doing here in Vermont? Of all the places in the world you could run to from Lower Bay—"

"This was the safest one I could think of," she answered without hesitation. "I remembered how it was when I came here to help you out on that case — dull, quiet, beautiful...and a great place to raise a child. And I thought I might be able to contact you through Sarah. I actually had no idea you were no longer in London." She paused. "My own life had become far from perfect, as you probably know pretty well by now."

Tyler suppressed a momentary twinge of guilt. "Go on."

"When — when things started to get really bad on Mustique with Kip, I discovered that I was willing to do anything," her voice took on a raspy, emotional quality, "anything to protect my son. When we finally ...escaped to Bequia, I had nothing, not even my own identity. But compared to the consequences of being found by Kip, it seemed a small price to pay for a semi–normal life. But then he and the band played at De Reef and Apoplexica started building their house in Friendship and I knew it was only a matter of time...I had to get us new passports and go somewhere no one would ever expect me to be. And that was when I thought of West Jordan."

Lucy paused for a moment, letting her gaze roam the humble surroundings. "When I contacted Sarah to see if she knew where you were, she didn't hesitate to invite me to come and stay here until I figured things out, even though we'd only met that one week nearly a decade ago. I had no idea they had three kids now or that she and Hunter had even lasted as a couple. But they have been so amazing, taking Tucker and me into their lives and making us feel so welcome." Her eyes filled with tears and Tyler found himself automatically reaching for her hand. She squeezed back appreciatively.

Then there was the sound of the downstairs door opening and lots of feet running up the stairs and down the hall and final three snow–suited figures followed by Hunter paraded noisily into the room.

With the lightning–fast reasoning of an experienced parent, Hunter quickly took charge of the situation. "Hey, guys, what d'you say we go down to the bar and order up a round of hot chocolates before dinner? We'll give these two a little more time to catch up before we invade."

"Yayyy!" And the children were gone before Tyler could completely absorb their presence.

""He's really good with them," Lucy commented. "You okay? Now where was I...oh right. So after Tucker and I got here, Sarah and I tried to locate you, but all we had was the address of a restaurant in Grenada. That was when I called a couple investigative journalist friends of mine to check up on you. I couldn't believe that the burned—out beachcomber they were describing was actually you until they showed me photos." Tyler shifted uncomfortably and released her hand, retreating to his end of the sofa.

"Sarah helped me concoct the scheme of how to get you to Bequia," she continued." We knew that independent as you are, you were going to have do your own climbing out of the hole you were in, and we could only hope that your real personality was still somewhere inside this new persona. We figured if we could get you to Lower Bay and get you intrigued by a challenging puzzle, you wouldn't be able to resist following it through. I emailed Ingrid and told her to be on the lookout for you, but apparently that wasn't necessary."

They shared a rueful smile about Ingrid and Tyler could see the relief on her face as she continued. "I wanted you to find us – but I couldn't bring myself to call you. Not after I'd made such a mess of your life."

He looked at her questioningly and she continued. "I should never have asked you to take over that Apoplexica story for me back in London. I felt sick for months when I heard about the car bombing. I tried to contact you back then but you had already fallen off the radar."

She turned to him then, her need for answers outweighing her uncertainty. "Tyler, what happened?"

So he told her, about his years in Grande Anse, about being continually haunted by the events outside his apartment in London, and how he'd succeeded in repressing everything until the call from "her sister." He told her about his time in Lower Bay with her friends, about going to Mustique to look for her, about Apoplexica and about the two weeks he spent adrift at sea. And then he told her about Old Year's Night and the bust in Friendship Bay and the arrests that were made and that Kip was out on bail but awaiting trial for possession of large quantities of illegal substances.

"And I don't think you are going to have worry about Kip bothering you anymore," he finished. "You can thank Calvin for that one."

Lucy was silent for a moment before appealing to him one last time. "Tyler, would you believe me if I told you it was never supposed to be as big a deal as it turned into? That you running into Ethan Sands and his band was never part of my agenda?"

"Yes," he said. "I believe you. And as ungrateful as I may sound, I am eternally thankful to you for whatever unorthodox means it took to resurrect my soul from the zombie I had become. And I hope someday in the future, that I will be of sound enough spirit to be reunited with my longtime companion, Mr. Mount Gay Rum." He gave a regretful laugh and then was immediately solemn. There was one more burning question that he did not know how to ask.

"Actually, love, my agenda is not at all complete yet." Lucy stood up and offered him a hand. "There's still a really important piece of it yet to happen. Come with me."

This time he did not protest when she led him towards the bar downstairs. The cozy glow of the wood–paneled room relaxed his very being in a long–forgotten way. He paused in the door to observe Sarah at work behind the polished wooden counter; age and motherhood had softened the angles of her lean limbs, sharpened the fine lines of her face and scattered long streaks of silver through her thick, dark tresses. The light in her eyes and her genuine smile assured him that the differences that had ended their relationship were behind her now.

"Welcome back, Tiger." She kissed his cheek and gave him a warm hug. "Lots of water under the bridge, huh?"

Before he could reply, Lucy called to him. "Tyler, over here." She was leaning against the fireplace, looking down at the oversized sofa where three kids with mugs of cocoa sat, their eyes riveted by a small TV that hung on the opposite wall.

He recognized the oldest one as Kashi, whom he had known as a golden–skinned refugee baby with corkscrew curls and who now, at nearly ten, displayed an ethereal preteen beauty. Next to her was Myles, the one who had scooted by him out to the car earlier. The third child had unruly blond hair and a round open face with a boldly freckled complexion; he sipped his cocoa but never took his tawny brown eyes off the cartoon characters that were running across the screen.

"Lucy, is–" he began but she cut him off.

"There's one more piece of the story you need to know." She pulled him aside, away from the fire into the dark entryway to the room. She took a deep breath. "I don't know any way to say this other than straight out. When I got pregnant..." She paused uncomfortably and then hurriedly continued. "Turns out Kip is sterile. I didn't know he couldn't have kids. When he discovered I was having a baby, he knew it wasn't his. He didn't throw me over, but he punished me any way he could. Over the years he became more and more abusive, to unreasonable and unacceptable levels. I..." Her voice broke and Tyler put a finger on her lips to stop her.

"You don't have to tell me. I know." Her confession confirmed what he had guessed many months before.

She smiled through her tears. "That night on the roof – I knew I was unprotected. It sounds perverse, I know, but I wanted you to get me pregnant. I knew you never wanted to have kids but I wanted to have your baby."

She pressed her face into his chest and finally, finally, he let himself feel what he'd been hoping and fearing since the day he opened the FedEx envelope and seen the photograph of the boy on the beach that reminded him so much of himself.

"Will you introduce me?" he whispered.

She nodded, wiping her eyes on his shirt. "Are you sure you're ready for this?"

"Do you think I scrimped and saved for months at Caribbean wages and then traveled for two days and nights just to see you?" He laughed.

Arm in arm, they walked back into the bar.

"Tucker. Tucker!" Lucy waved her arm in front of his face to get his attention. Reluctantly, the boy turned his gaze away from the television and looked curiously at Tyler. "There's somebody I'd like you to meet."

ABOUT THE AUTHOR

A lifelong lover of travel, mysteries and creative expression, Marilinne Cooper has always enjoyed the escapist pleasure of combining her passions in a good story. She lives in the White Mountains of New Hampshire and is also a freelance copywriting professional. To learn more, visit marilinnecooper.com.

ALSO BY MARILINNE COOPER

Night Heron
Butterfly Tattoo
Blue Moon
Double Phoenix
Dead Reckoning
Snake Island
Windfall

Jamaican Draw

DATE DUE			
DEC 2 1 2017			
APR 2 3 2018			
DEC 1 1 2018			

CPSIA information can be obtained
at www.ICGtesting.com
Printed in the USA
LVOW10s1645191117
556906LV00012B/756/P

9 781507 524527